WALKING
THE RIM

WALKING
THE RIM

by Susan Hart Lindquist

CAROLINE HOUSE
BOYDS MILLS PRESS

To my children,
Charlie, Maddy, and Sam,
and to old friends and old dogs--
may some things never change.

--S.H.L.

Text copyright © 1992 by Susan Hart Lindquist
Illustrations copyright © 1992 by Boyds Mills Press

Published by Caroline House
Boyds Mills Press, Inc.
A Highlights Company
910 Church Street
Honesdale, Pennsylvania 18431

Publisher Cataloging-in-Publication Data
Lindquist, Susan Hart.
  Walking the rim / by Susan Hart Lindquist.
[144] p. : ill. ; cm.
Summary: A family summer camping trip turns into a true-life adventure
when an earthquake separates Rudy from his parents.
ISBN 1-56397-098-8
1. Adventure stories—Juvenile literature. [1. Adventure stories.] I. Title.
[F]   1992
Library of Congress Catalog Card Number: 91-76966

First edition, 1992
Book designed by Tim Gillner
The text of this book is set in 11-point Bookman Light.
Distributed by St. Martin's Press
Printed in the United States of America

10 9 8 7 6 5 4 3 2 1

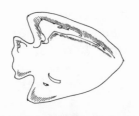

Prologue

There was no path for us to follow except the one my grandfather made, his unhurried strides flattening the damp shadowed grass ahead of me, his arm sweeping aside low fir branches long enough for me to pass.

I'd been eagerly tagging along after him all morning, forcing myself to walk slowly, the way he did.

"Don't charge over the ground like a rolling boulder," he whispered. "Hurry too much and you might step over a golden opportunity."

I think I loved exploring with Papa D more than anything else in the world. Over the years he'd taught me where to hunt for fossils along the riverbank, and how to find licorice root in the moss on the buckeye trees. And he always brought notice to things I'd overlooked before, like the way swallows fly low at twilight, skimming over the water to catch bugs before the fish do.

That day we were hiking uphill, walking along the

ridge above a narrow creek looking for bobcat tracks. For a long time we'd been walking freely, only having to duck beneath an occasional tree limb or slide around a clump of brush now and then. But finally we came to a spot where our way was blocked by a wide thicket of brambles, and it was obvious that we couldn't go on without crossing to the other side of the ravine.

"We'll have to cross here," Papa D said, pointing to a log that bridged the gully.

He was already on the other side by the time I worked up enough nerve to look over the edge. The creek bed lay open below me like the jaws of a hungry monster.

"I can't. . . ." My words teetered the way I was sure that old tree would. "It's too high."

My grandfather just sent me a solid stare from the other side.

"I'll do it if you hold my hand," I said.

Papa D chuckled as he stepped out onto the log. I thought he was coming to get me, but he wasn't.

Instead, he stopped halfway over and began to rock back and forth, putting all the force of his weight into trying to show me that the log wouldn't fall. "Solid as the ground you're standing on," he said. "Come on. You won't fall if you don't look down. Walk to me, Rudy. Do it alone this time, and it will be easy on the way back."

That was five years ago. I was only eight then, and thinking back on it, the drop couldn't have been much. Even if I had fallen, I probably wouldn't have gotten hurt. But that log scared me so badly that I sat down in the dirt and wouldn't budge.

Papa D never let me get too close to tears over anything, especially when I was afraid, and he knew high places made me nervous. He waited for a moment, then walked back across the log. Smiling, he reached into his pocket and pulled out the arrowhead he always carried. "What you need is a little more faith, boy," he said, holding it out to me.

I don't remember crossing that log—something about his putting the arrowhead into my hand took the worry right out of me. All I recall is that when I reached the other side and tried to give it back to him, he shook his head. "No, Son," he said. "You hang on to that. You're probably going to need it again someday."

From that day on, whenever he saw me, Papa D would ask if I still had "that old rock." I'd pull it out to show him, and he'd grin. "Men search all their lives for these small pieces of faith," he would say, turning the arrowhead over in his hand. "But don't be mistaken. I didn't give it to you for luck. Whatever you do, Rudy, don't be fooled. There's no such thing as luck."

Chapter *1*

Wedged in the back seat of the van between a stack of camping gear and my dog, I should have been excited. But I wasn't. Something told me that a vacation without Papa D was going to be as boring as homework.

My father climbed into the driver's seat and flipped the shades up on his wire-rimmed glasses. Then he turned to survey the rest of us. He stiffened as Smithers settled beside me. "I hope we won't be sorry we didn't board that animal at the kennel."

Smithers licked my cheek and draped a floppy paw across my leg. He was a yellow lab, almost a year old and big by then, but still stupid enough to be a nuisance. My dad couldn't stand him. He thought dogs should have better manners than people, and if they didn't, they ought to be left at home.

"Relax, Jim." Mom gave Dad a gentle nudge as he backed the van out of the driveway. "Smithers'll be fine. The woods will be a great change for him. There's nothing he can get into way out there."

My mother was right. Our campsite was miles from the nearest town, back in the hills. In California we call them hills. Almost anywhere else they'd be mountains.

Dad turned the corner at the end of our street and headed for the freeway. He glanced at me in the rearview mirror as Smithers fidgeted on the seat beside me. I could tell it was going to be a long two weeks.

"I think we'd better stop to see Papa D before we leave town. . . ." Dad took a right toward Valley Memorial Hospital.

My stomach lurched. It was noon on a warm summer day, but inside I was suddenly as cold as the Pacific Ocean.

I couldn't bear to look out the window; I already knew what was there. Oak trees shaded the front terrace, and old folks' chairs lined the railing.

And the building was white, just like everything else when you are old and sick. I wondered what made people think that just because Papa D had had a stroke, he didn't want a little color in his life.

"He won't go in, Mama," my six-year-old brother Wade announced. "Rudy doesn't love Papa D anymore."

"Of course Rudy loves his grandfather"—my mother leaned over the seat and reached past my sister Deena to pat Wade's knee. "We all do." Her smile was too kind. It made me feel small.

Wade knew what he was talking about, of course. And even though I had the arrowhead in my pocket, I knew that this time probably wouldn't be any different from the other times I had been brought to visit Papa D.

I had seen him only once since his stroke, and that was in May, when they first moved him from the regular hospital. Since then, I hadn't been able to get any farther than the lobby.

It wasn't as if I didn't try. I would always go in, and I'd

make it as far as the elevators before my legs quit working and I froze, knotted up by an urgent case of stomach cramps.

"Honestly, Rudy." Dad rolled down the window halfway and slid open the van's side door. "I don't know what your problem is. You and your grandfather used to be such good friends."

Yes. The best of friends. But now a hole bored inside me every time I thought of Papa D. I guess it was like ulcers, but worse—no one had invented a medicine for the way I felt.

"Come along, Son," Dad said, urging me with a pat on the shoulder. "It won't be so bad. Papa D's much better. He'll be up and around in no time, good as new. The nurses assure me he'll be in a wheel chair by next week."

Just once, I wished my father would look me in the eye and talk truthfully about how sick Papa D really was.

But when Dad spoke about him, his words were carefully chosen and hopeful, as if my grandfather had simply broken his arm or bumped his head.

"You realize, don't you, that while we're gone your grandfather won't have any visitors? It's about time you came face to face with your problem. Think of Papa D's feelings for a change. . . ."

"Take it easy, Jim," Mom said. "He'll see Papa D soon. When he's ready. Often these things take time." She tried to put her arm around me then, but I stepped away. "I know your grandfather misses you, Rudy. I see it in his eyes."

Who did Mom think she was fooling? How could she see anything in Papa D's eyes? The only time I saw him after his stroke, his eyes had been as blank as two gray stones.

Wade and Deena climbed out of the van. Dad paused on the sidewalk to unsnap the camera case that was hanging around his neck.

It wasn't bad enough that we had to stop at the hospital on the way out of town. Dad had to line us up like a flower arrangement right there in the parking lot in front of the whole world and take one of his famous "before" pictures—as if he expected us to come back from the trip three feet taller, with me shaving and my sister Deena with boobs or something.

"We'll save the picture for Papa D." Dad beamed. "He'll love it." Everyone said "cheese," and as quick as that, Dad wrapped up his camera, snapped the case, looked at his watch, and turned to lead us up the marigold-lined walk to the hospital.

Mom marched ahead of me, her purse slung over her arm, her blonde hair brushing her collar. For my mother, visiting Papa D seemed as easy as making a trip to the grocery store.

Deena and Wade kept up with her. My sister Deena was eleven and thought she was the queen of the world.

The automatic doors whooshed open, and we entered the air-conditioned lobby.

"Old people smell bad," Wade whispered. "It stinks in here."

There was hardly a sound as we passed the reception desk, only the dull green carpet scrunching under our feet like dead leaves.

Mom caught up with Dad and ran her hand over his back. How come he had to pretend that Papa D's stroke didn't make him sad? I knew it did. Right then I could tell by the way the stripes on his shirt tightened across his back as he walked. I followed them, but my heart jumped in my throat so badly that by the time we reached the elevators I had to stuff my hands into my pockets to keep them from shaking.

My arrowhead was still there. I gripped it tightly, but I knew it wasn't going to do me any good. No matter how hard I tried, I wasn't going to make it.

8

"I have to go to the bathroom," I choked as the doors sucked open in front of me. "You go ahead. I'll wait out here."

As I sat alone in the lobby waiting for the visit to end, I fought hard to remember how Papa D used to be—the way he was in the picture I kept hidden in my pocket. It had been stuck in the mirror over his dresser in the old house, and when no one was in the room, I'd taken it.

The day they closed up Papa D's house in Stockton, the whole family showed up to sort through his belongings. It was as if he'd already died, the way the relatives couldn't wait to jump in and pick over his things. Not just the big stuff, like the furniture that my aunt and uncle got their hands on, but personal things, too: his pipes, his fishing tackle, even the junk in his bathroom. It gave me the creeps; it seemed that since his stroke my grandfather had become only a piece of furniture, too.

The picture was one he'd taken of the two of us the last time we went fishing. I never looked at it much, unless I was alone. It made me too sad.

I remember my grandfather shouting as he bounded toward me over the rocky shore. "You got it, Rudy? That's a big one! Hold tight!"

The trout yanked on my line, thrashing at the river's edge while I waited for Papa D to catch up. He knelt beside me as I pulled the hook from the fish's mouth.

"He swallowed it." I cringed, trying not to bring too much flesh with the hook.

"I'd say he's a good twelve inches, wouldn't you? Biggest I've seen in this part of the river since I was a kid."

I reached for the bag to toss it in. I knew my fish wasn't any bigger than the three he'd caught the day before. He was just trying to make me feel important.

"Hold on, there. I've got to have a picture of this."

9

Papa D put the camera on a log a couple of feet in front of us and set the shutter so he could run back and slide into the picture beside me. "Say 'sidewinder'," he told me, grabbing me around the shoulder. "Hold that sucker high. Got to make that fish look as big as we can!" I held up my scrawny trout as if it were a first-place trophy.

The clock jumped. I wanted to be outside with Smithers, away from the critical glances of the receptionist, away from the biting smells of the hospital. But I ignored them and pulled the picture out of my pocket. Staring at it, I tried to remember just how that day had smelled, how the breeze had felt on my face, how Papa D's hand had felt on my shoulder.

In the photograph, the wisps of white hair on the top of Papa D's almost-bald head stood straight up in the wind like a fan. Nearly his whole face was a smile in the picture. It was a happy, healthy face, hearty and tough as saddle leather. Back then, it never crossed my mind that anything bad could ever happen to Papa D. Nothing short of dying—which I was sure would come like a brilliant flash, quick and clean. I'd practiced for that, sure I would be lots older and ready for it by the time it happened.

When Dad and the rest of the family finally rounded the corner and started down the hallway, it took me only a few seconds to get up and out to the parking lot. Smithers was waiting impatiently, his wet snout sticking out of the window. "Hey, boy," I said. He licked my face as I got to the door.

Out of the corner of my eye, I saw Dad cup his hands around his mouth. "Don't let that blasted dog out!" he yelled. "He'll get himself run over!"

"Sure, Dad," I said. I wondered what made him think I'd ever let anything happen to the best friend I had left in the world.

Chapter 2

Smithers stirred beside me, his toe-nails grating against one of the blue nylon sleeping bags.

"Take it easy with that dog back there," Dad warned. "Don't let him get into anything." He picked me out in the rearview mirror to make sure he had my attention before he went on.

"I thought I'd get an early start on a hike upriver tomorrow. Try to locate that old fishing hole. You know the one, Rudy—where Papa D took us last summer? It shouldn't be too hard to find."

Why did it feel as if Dad was trying to make me miss Papa D more than I already did? I quit listening and turned to watch out the window.

Right then I didn't think my father would be able to find anything, unless it was in a book with maps and instructions and dotted lines to follow. He just didn't have the same instincts as my grandfather.

Dad was so organized that he had an itinerary for our

whole trip set up before we even backed out of the driveway. He planned for absolutely everything: what time we'd go fishing, what time we'd eat breakfast, what we'd eat, where we'd hike if it was sunny, what we'd do if it rained. He kept it all listed in a little leather book in the zippered pocket of his jacket.

I stared out the window, watching dust skirts kick up from the tires as we left the main highway. My reflection waved faintly against the hot glass, my face fading in and out, then disappearing altogether as we drove deeper into the trees.

We came out of the woods onto the high wind-combed ridge above the river. From there the water was only a pale green ribbon at the bottom of the valley, winding like a snake over the gray rocky riverbed. During the winter rains it swelled and surged over the riverbank, carrying logs and fallen trees as if they were toothpicks. But in the summer it was only a shallow stream, about thirty feet across and never past my shoulders in the deepest parts.

On our side of the river, the land was open rangeland for sheep and cattle. But on the other side, the hills were dark and shadowy, cloaked in ancient stands of old growth timber.

A narrow bridge crossed the river at the bottom of the hill. I knew people lived on the other side, because on cold, windless mornings smoke trails rose from the woods over there. My parents and Papa D knew some of them, but we never went to visit.

***

I'd intended to ask Dad if he wanted to go fishing after we set up the tents, but I gave up my plan when he unfolded a canvas camp chair and sat down.

12

"You kids walk to the river and scout around," he said, checking his watch. "Snap to it, though. It'll be dark soon. And, Rudy, take your dog, but for Pete's sake, don't lose track of him." Dad paused for a moment to make sure I was listening. "By the way," he went on, "I'm laying down the law. If that dog of yours takes it into his mind to run off and chase wildlife, under no circumstances are you to go after him."

"Your dad's right," said my mother. "You and Smithers might come across a local rancher with a gun. Nobody tolerates dogs pestering livestock around here." She opened a chair beside Dad. "Deena, I expect you to come home dry. No frog chasing this late in the day."

With that, Deena and Wade took off at a run across the field toward the willow-lined riverbank. I knew my brother and sister weren't remembering that the year before Papa D had been the one who went with us to the river on the first day. My grandfather had been strong then, strong enough to carry Wade on his shoulders and hike all day long with me.

The yellowing grass crackled beneath my shoes and sent grasshoppers jumping in front of me like popcorn. With his nose to the ground and his tail pointed high, Smithers darted in and out of the brush, surprising quail. They rose in angry flapping clouds around him as he circled back to prance beside me. He was eager for a run after the long ride, so I let him spring ahead to catch up with Wade and Deena. I didn't feel like playing with him anyway.

The wind blew hard through the valley in the late afternoon, pushing up from the ocean cold gray fingers of fog that wrapped around the trees like woolly gloves. It was Papa D's favorite time of day.

Every evening before sunset he and I used to climb up the hill to watch the hawks hunt, red-tailed and Cooper's, circling wide over the grassy hillside.

13

The summer before we had discovered a pair of golden eagles that flew in from the north every night. Their dark, broad, powerful wings had swept the air like deep breaths, carrying them the width of the valley into the treetops on the other side of the river.

Eagles fly higher than hawks. They climb on rising thermals and circle there, spiraling down slowly when they spot their prey. Then they tuck their wings in tight against their bodies, turning themselves into giant black Ws that suddenly tip forward as if they've lost their balance and shoot straight to the ground like heavy stones.

I searched the graying sky, but there were no eagles that evening. A breeze blew down from the hills, bringing with it the sweet-spicy smell of alder trees. A cluster of swallows swooped up, scattered, and pulled together again, black and fast. A fish jumped, a stick bobbed along in the current, and leaves skipped over the rocks before circling in on themselves in a tiny whirlpool against the rocky bank.

That summer, and for all the summers that I remember, there had been a high bank of sword ferns on the other side of the river. They climbed the hillside for thirty feet or so, then mingled with the madrone and alders that grew low on the hills.

But the riverbank had changed in a year's time. All the ferns were gone. Small landslides had pulled down the bank and covered it with broken pepperwood branches and deadwood from fallen trees. It was grim and ugly, and even as I was standing there, the ground seemed to shudder as stray rocks slid down the slope to the water.

Shivering, I took out my arrowhead. It was a small one, not even a quarter the size of my hand. I think it must have been remembering Papa D just then that made it feel suddenly heavy, like the tears waiting to come behind my eyes.

My mother was forever telling me to quit feeling sorry for myself, that the whole world had troubles and mine were the smallest kind. I knew feeling bad wouldn't help, but at that moment some part of me wanted to bring back the pain that sneaked up inside me every time I thought about Papa D. It was like needing to go back for a second sniff at a bad smell. The sadness had a sweetness about it that made me want to feel it over and over again.

I faced downriver into the wind, which ruffled the surface of the water and whisked over the rocks toward me. I swung with it as it came, turning to see Deena kneeling by the water and Smithers racing along the shore with Wade, who was waving and laughing. Although I could tell Smithers was barking, I couldn't hear him. The wind carried the sounds away from me.

I knew if I didn't round them up, they'd stay at the river until dark; then I'd be the one to catch the blame. In that way they were like Smithers, still like little kids. When they were playing, they forgot about everything else. Right then I felt almost grown, because I couldn't seem to do that anymore.

Wade had hold of Smithers's collar and was signaling me to hurry up. He was trying to keep him out of the water.

"What's the matter?" I shouted over the wind.

"I can't hold him. He sees something."

"Give him here," I said, panting as I clattered over the rocks to reach them. "He's going to pull you into the water if you're not careful."

A growl rose from deep in Smithers's throat as he stopped and turned to look across the river. The short yellow hairs rose along his spine. His flanks quivered.

I looped my finger through the ring on his collar and gave him a firm jerk. Reluctantly, Smithers sat down beside my feet. "Stay!" I bellowed, out of breath.

Smithers looked up at me as if I'd betrayed him. He wasn't a dumb dog. He just had his own mind about what he wanted to do. My deep-down wish was that he'd be so stuck to me he wouldn't ever want to run off, like dogs on TV shows that save kids' lives or walk them to school and wait outside till they're done and then walk them home again.

"Bad dog!" I yanked on his collar again. Yelling at him made me feel like a heel, so I let go to scratch his ears.

"Stay," I repeated halfheartedly. His tail brushed the pebbles behind him from side to side. He was good for just about one second.

Then, like a rocket he was gone. Practically flying toward the water, he jumped into the stream with a terrific splash.

Deena had been crouching gingerly at the shore, investigating the shallow water, careful not to let even her feet get wet till then. She had resisted the temptation to scoop up polliwogs by keeping her hands deep in her pockets. With her hands that way, she couldn't balance herself, and as Smithers raced by her, she rolled over in one smooth motion, her feet following her shoulders in a head-first spin into the river.

By the time Smithers reached midstream, Deena was sitting waist-deep in the water, drenched from the top of her head to the seat of her pants.

Mindless of the trouble he'd caused, Smithers bounded on, taking the slippery rocks one at a time, zigzagging his way across the river. When he reached the other side, he shook the water off his back and plopped down, still wagging his tail.

"Mom will have a fit!" Deena moaned. "I'm soaked."

"No doubt about that." I couldn't help laughing as I leaned to give her a hand. "You look like a wet sock."

She stood up to her knees in the river, dripping wet and trying not to laugh. "I'm freezing," she wailed. "It isn't funny!" Her sweatshirt sagged, and when she stepped on shore, her shoes squished and little spurts of water shot out of them. Wade and I went into hysterics.

It never seems fair that it's usually the things that make you laugh the hardest that get you in the most trouble. Though Mom might scold Deena a little for getting dumped in the river, Dad was going to kill me for not holding onto Smithers.

Suddenly Wade tugged on my sleeve. "What's that?" he whispered, pointing downriver.

"What's *what?*"

"That, over there. See?"

I squinted my eyes and looked across the river, but the woods on the other side were already hidden by evening shadows.

"I saw something," Wade said again. "Over there in the bushes."

Chapter
3

"It was probably just a deer," said Deena. She was standing in the wind, her teeth chattering. "Let's go. I'm cold."

All I could make out downriver were dim outlines of tree trunks and underbrush. "Nothing's moving, Wade. Whatever it was, it's gone now. We'd better go back. Where's Smithers?"

"He's over there, on the other side."

We all turned to look upriver toward the place where Smithers had been lying, but he was gone.

"What happened to him? Where'd he go?—Smithers!" I swung around and grabbed Wade's arm. "I thought you said he was over there. Did you see him or not?" I spun in a circle and called him again.

"I don't know where he went." Wade yanked away from me. "Don't get mad. It isn't my fault if he won't come when you call!"

"There he is," Deena said softly, under her breath. "Look at him—he's just standing there."

A distance up the beach on the other side of the river, Smithers stood with his nose in the air, frozen like a bronze statue.

"What's he doing?" asked Wade, stepping close to me.

Deena shrugged. "He probably smells that deer. Call him back, Rudy. I'm cold."

Smithers was a good ways upriver from us. Even so, I could see the ridge of hairs lined high on his back. He'd caught the scent of something, all right, but before I had a chance to say a word, he dashed across the sandbank and disappeared into the woods.

"SMITHERS!" I shrieked as I caught a final glimpse of his yellow tail vanishing in the trees. "I'll have to go after him. If I show up without him, Dad'll murder me."

Deena touched my arm. Her hand was wet and cold. "Don't go, Rudy. He'll come back."

She called for him then, sending her voice ringing up and down the riverbank. We waited in silence for a moment; then we all tried calling together. But I knew it was hopeless. Smithers had never answered to his name before. Why should he do it now?

"Tell them I'll be back by dinner," I said as I headed for the river. "Tell them I took Smithers for a walk. Tell them anything. I don't care."

I wasn't two steps into the water before I looked back and saw Wade high-tailing it past Deena toward camp to tell Dad what I was doing.

The water spun slowly around my knees as I worked my way over the mossy rocks on the river bottom. All I needed now was to dump myself into the water and show up back at camp drenched to the bone—with no Smithers. It was going to be hard enough to explain how I'd gotten my shoes and pants wet.

I called him again as I climbed onto the opposite shore, praying he'd show up before my father did. Then, from behind me on the other side of the river, I heard

Dad calling my name. By his tone I could tell he wasn't pleased.

"Which way did he go, Son?" I turned to see him waving impatiently at me to come back. He lifted his binoculars to scan the forested hill above me.

I trudged back through the water and joined him.

Lowering the field glasses, he rested his hands on his hips. "I thought I told you not to chase after that dog," he said quietly, almost whispering. The wind picked up his words and swept them away.

Dad whistled for Smithers, and I called. After about ten minutes he stopped. "There's no point in spending the night doing this. If your dog intends to return, it isn't going to be our calling him that'll do it. Think we'll have to give up for tonight."

"But, Dad . . ."

"It will be dark soon, anyway. If he gets hungry, he'll make his own way home. The road cuts back to the Matheson place on the other side of the ridge. We'll drive out there in the morning and look for him if he doesn't return by then."

In long, deliberate strides my father walked a few feet ahead of me, his steps carefully placed so he wouldn't kick up any dirt. I could tell he was trying to control his anger. Everything about him looked tense, wound like a rattlesnake ready to strike.

"I hope for your sake that dog comes back soon." He slowed to wait for me. "He was depending on you to look after him, you know."

I hesitated on the path, then let Dad go ahead of me. I watched him take those long, dustless strides and found myself scuffing at the ground as noisily as I could.

"It wasn't my fault," Deena wailed, back at camp, still trying to explain why she had shown up soaked through to her underwear.

"It was Rudy," said Wade, running up to Dad. "He let

Smithers go and he knocked Deena over."

Mom had a towel and was industriously rubbing Deena's hair. "Maybe you should have been holding onto Smithers instead of being so close to the water, young lady. I don't think this is anyone's fault except mine. I never should have allowed you to go down there." She looked up at Dad and me. "Did you find him?"

I shook my head, unable to look her in the eye, half-worried about how they intended to punish me, half-worried about Smithers. The thought of losing him made my chest ache, as if a rubber band was wrapped around it.

"Smithers will be fine," Mom said. "He'll come back, you'll see." She finished with Deena's head and gave her a little swat on the bottom. "You and Rudy have dry clothes. Scoot off to the tent and get dressed."

"Wait a minute," said Dad, holding up his hand. "Stand over here and let me get a shot of this before you change."

No matter what, my dad wasn't going to miss this chance for another "family snap." Even though there was hardly any daylight left, he trotted into the tent and came back with his camera, screwed on a special lens, and set us up in that familiar line.

"This is great!" He grinned and peered into the viewfinder. "We'll take this home to show Papa D. He'll get a bang out of this one. Now, all of you stand together, and 'smile!'"

There we were again, the three of us—me half-covered in river mud; Deena in her wet clothes, her teeth knocking together and her sweatshirt drooping to her knees; and Wade, smiling as usual, with a graham cracker already shoved in his mouth.

And there was Dad. I was sure he'd already forgotten about Smithers as he stood pointing at us in his clean socks and ironed khaki shorts.

It was hard to figure how he could be so different from Papa D, so perfectly put together, and still be his son. My grandfather never gave a hoot about whether his shirt was tucked in or if his hair was combed just so. As Dad signaled for us to keep still while he adjusted the lens on his camera, it occurred to me that if Papa D had been there, he would have crossed the river to help me look for Smithers.

***

As soon as we finished dinner, Dad took out his black book.

"What's on the agenda for the morning, Jim?" Mom said, passing the bag of marshmallows around the campfire.

"Obviously, not what I'd planned. I guess I'll have to take a ride over to the Mathesons' if the dog's not back." He flipped the pages of his book nervously with his thumb.

"Good," said Mom. "And Rudy can go with you. You remember Colleen's got her sister's children now."

"You bet he'll go with me." Dad closed the book and jabbed the fire with a stick. Sparks squirted over his head, hot as his temper. "He'll go with me. And if that dog is there, Rudy will be the one to explain how he came to be lost. If I know Jack Matheson and that partner of his, neither of them is going to appreciate a stray dog showing up on their property."

Chapter
4

Fog dampened the early evening, bringing all of us close to the fire. I couldn't get Smithers off my mind. Everything outside the circle of firelight was black, hollow, and bottomless. The wind ran through the forest and sucked the fog down from the treetops. It crept along the ground, skirting the flames like a draft across an empty room. It swept cold along my back.

Mom brought blankets, and we all wrapped up for a while until Wade began to yawn and she declared bedtime. No one had said a word about Smithers. I was sure they had forgotten all about him.

As the others followed the lantern beam to the tents, Dad slid his chair up close to me. "I'd like to talk to you about what happened today," he said, anchoring his hand on my shoulder the way he did when he had something important he wanted to say. But right then it felt like his hand was positioning me for an ambush. I was sure he was going to tear into me about losing

Smithers. But he didn't.

"I'm disappointed that you wouldn't join us at the hospital this afternoon. Your grandfather really seemed to light up when we visited him. You know, Son, it must break his heart that you don't go in to see him."

Even though Papa D was his father and only my grandfather, it bothered me when Dad acted as if he knew him better than I did. I couldn't listen anymore, and I pulled away, suddenly repelled by the weight of his hand on my shoulder. Without turning to look at him, I stood up and followed the others toward the shelter of the tent.

Inside, silhouettes from the campfire danced on the wall of the tent, and I tried to fall asleep to the murmur of my parents' voices as they sat beside the fire. There in the darkness, it was a reassuring sound.

Beside me, where Smithers should have been, Wade slept peacefully, only his mass of blond hair showing out of the top of his sleeping bag.

Deena was curled up against the farthest wall of the tent, finally asleep after having made a lot of fuss about me hogging the extra blanket. She said she wished she could sleep in a separate tent, without any boys. I told her she was welcome to trade places with Smithers—wherever he was.

As I lay in the dark, staring up at the top of the tent, I began to pick up bits of my parents' conversation. I could tell what they were discussing by the troubled tone of their words. The shadows jumped, and I knew my dad was poking the coals of the fire as he spoke.

"First that nonsense with his grandfather, and now that dog. What's the matter with the boy, anyway?"

The glow on the wall of the tent flared brilliant yellow and lit up the night outside so well I could see the bowed line of my father's back as he leaned over the fire.

He didn't wait for Mom to answer. "The least he could

do would be to go in and see him. That waiting in the lobby business has to stop. It's not as if I'm expecting that much. . . ."

I let the song of the river spilling over the rocks cover Dad's words. I tried to imagine the frogs hiding in the damp grass, the birds nesting high in the trees, the trout asleep at the bottom of the river.

But each new picture faded into a vision of Papa D and the way he looked the only time I'd visited him in the hospital, thin and gray with hollow eyes and parchment skin. I tried not to think about him, tried to shove him out of my mind into the place where I usually kept that memory. But my brain made images of him all by itself, bad visions of him laid flat out and staring at me from the bed in that white room, not watching anything, not seeing. But the whole time I felt as if his eyes were set on me, waiting—as if he was begging me to do something, say something, explain what had happened to him, while my father just went on talking.

But I couldn't. For me, it was like walking on the edge of a high cliff. I couldn't speak, afraid I'd slip and say something wrong, as if my words would damage Papa D even more. My father just went on talking to the sterile air in that room, pretending everything was fine, and waiting for me to do the same.

Without my telling it to, the fear made my body go all kinds of crazy inside. Panic cramped my stomach, and I shrank back, unable to touch my grandfather's hand, to look at his face or in his eyes, and I turned and ran from the room.

Blinking against the memory, I closed my eyes again, only to fall into a vision of Smithers, with his belly laid bare by the claw of some predator, his eyes fixed accusingly on me.

After a while I heard Dad shovel dirt over the fire. It spit and popped as it began to cool, and the night went black. In the emptiness, I found myself wishing my parents had stayed up until I had fallen asleep.

Somewhere in the distance the high-pitched cry of a nighthawk broke the stillness. A bitter sound, sharp and lonely, it pierced the silence like an icy needle.

Still unable to close my eyes, I lay awake and listened as one by one nighttime noises began to fill the woods outside the tent. Brush stirred under the footsteps of passing deer. Something scratched at a tree trunk. A fox called. Raccoons chattered. And all the frogs in the river woke up to sing at the same time.

But behind all of it, as I lay in the warmth of the tent, I imagined I could hear Smithers's unhappy whine, and I wondered if he was cold.

Chapter
5

Reaching around blindly, I felt for my jeans, then quietly pulled myself out of my sleeping bag and slipped them on.

The racket of the darkness sank into a hush as I crawled from the tent into the night air. Every living creature quieted.

A three-quarter moon was rising above the hills. Ghostlike, it backlit the jagged outline of the ridge on the other side of the river where Smithers had disappeared. It spread a shadowy blanket of light across our campground—enough for me to see where I was going. But the river seemed miles away, only a black ripple against the trees. Silver reflections flickered along the top of the water where it rounded the corner at the base of the hill.

I tried to ignore the creeping sensation that I was being followed, and began to walk toward the river. It was a feeling I always got in open spaces, as if something or someone was sneaking up on me, ready to put a cold hand, or a claw, on my neck. A shadow passed over my head as the silhouette of an owl crossed the night sky. I swung around, not really expecting to see anything behind me, not really afraid, but making sure.

"A little late to be taking a walk, isn't it?" My mother's stern whisper rode the darkness between us. The beam of her flashlight caught me, turning the night around me as black as the bottom of the ocean.

"I thought I heard Smithers," I lied.

"It's too cold to be wandering around. Smithers will be just fine. Get back to bed before your dad wakes up. And for heaven's sake, don't disturb the others."

Mom flipped off the flashlight and disappeared into her tent but not before I heard my father's irritated words. "Don't tell me he's out looking for that damn dog."

***

It must have been close to dawn when the soft padding of feet circling the tent woke me. It was too quiet to be the middle of the night. Even the raccoons had gone back to sleep. The footsteps stopped outside, close to my head. A sniff . . . a whine . . .

I scrambled in the dark to find my pants and shoes.

Smithers licked me in the face and wagged his rear end, ready to play. "It's the middle of the night, for Pete's sake, you dumb dog." I reached for his collar, but he scooted away to sniff the ground. He was looking for a stick for me to throw.

"Get over here!" My whisper was harsh against the heavy stillness outside the tent. Patting my leg some-times worked to coax him, so I gave it a try. But he backed away.

I called softly, but he went on ignoring me. Somehow I had to get hold of him. "Here, boy," I tried again and knelt to grab him. He backed away and stared at me for a moment, then hunkered down on his front legs and imitated me, his tail going ninety miles an hour. He was daring me to go after him.

"Good boy. Here, Smithers." I tried patting the dirt, but nothing worked. Stupid dog. Didn't he know I was trying to help him?

Then all at once, something caught his attention. He didn't growl. He didn't bark. He didn't make a sound. His ears stood up, he turned his head, and his nose climbed the breeze.

"No, boy," I said. "Here, Smithers." But I moved too quickly toward him, and his tail turned, his nose dove into the dirt, and he took off following an invisible trail into the night.

"Smithers . . . come back. . . ." My words were nothing more than a dry rattle lost in my throat.

The ashes of the campfire were as cold as gravel and as silent as my parents asleep in the tent behind me. The sound of my sneakers beating the dust was the only thing I could hear, except for my own struggle to catch my breath. I was almost to the river before I realized what I had done. Stopping just short of the willows, I listened for him. I could barely make out his shadow about twenty feet away, slithering toward the water. He was pacing fast up and down the shore, his hind feet scattering small stones as he ran. For a moment I heard his high, frustrated whimper echo eerily against the opposite bank. Then he splashed into the water and broke for the other side.

"Smi—*thers*!" I called, desperation choking my cry as I stepped into the water.

The current swirled around my ankles, up my calves, and past my knees. Cringing, I dug my fingernails into my palms, struggling to keep my balance as the soles of my shoes slid over the rocky river bottom.

By the time I got to the other side, my jeans were soaked to my thighs, and against the hill Smithers was only a faint shadow, almost as dark as the trees.

I fixed my eyes on the ground and began to grope across the moonlit shore. Somewhere ahead of me the brush rustled. Smithers was already far past the beach and on his way up the hill.

I heard him again when I reached the cover of the trees. He'd gone up a small ravine where Papa D took me last summer looking for trilliums. With a shudder, I remembered we had followed the stream that ran through the canyon until we couldn't go any farther— and it had taken us almost a whole day to do it.

I took a deep breath, rubbed my arrowhead for luck, then stepped into the icy water of the creek. As I did, Papa D's words came back to me. "Remember, Rudy, there's no such thing as luck."

On our hike last summer, the creek bed had been cool and peaceful. That day it had been full of beauty and mystery, but now it was a different world. Down there in the dark, it was as cold and as cavernous as a nightmare.

And the air was different, too—moist and pungent. Green smells of damp earth were sucked into my nostrils. I crouched to make my way beneath a thick growth of brambles. Climbing briers grabbed my shirt and yanked my pants as I began to crawl, crablike, up the rocky stream.

The forest howled and whistled and screeched. Something swift and black moved through the branches of the trees and settled a few feet above my head.

Almost blindly, I splashed from pool to pool, feeling my way up and over the rocks that lined the narrow twisting canyon. No moonlight reached that deep into the trees. I hugged a wet boulder and wedged my foot in a cranny to boost myself up. "Smithers!" I yelled, startled by the sound of my own voice.

Smithers's howl floated down to me, and I climbed on, without regard for where he was leading me, too afraid to look back. Hanging limbs of alder trees scraped across my face and snatched at my hair. I lost my footing on a mossy rock, slipped, and fell backwards into the water, scraping my ankle raw on a jagged rock at the bottom. But I ignored the pain. I was too scared to let it stop me.

Step by step, I continued to climb, but more slowly, until the walls of the ravine wrapped me inside a space no wider than the spread of my arms.

Through the tops of the trees the sky began to lighten. Morning was coming, but as I went on, the canyon gradually gave way to an overgrown jungle, and I fell with nearly each step, sinking to my waist in ferns that clutched my legs like huge, wet hands.

Finally I had to stop. Ten feet in front of me my way was blocked by an enormous Douglas fir that had fallen across the canyon.

Exhausted, I shinnied up onto the fallen log to see if I could go on, but beyond me there was only an impassable wall of snags and brush. I called for Smithers with all my might. Overhead, the waking birds left their roosts and yelled back at me. Again and again, my voice echoed off the rim of the canyon, but there was no sign of Smithers anywhere.

I wanted to cry, and all at once my body was flooded with the pain that I had passed over on my dash up the ravine. My ankle throbbed. Swollen and already going purple, it was caked with drying blood. My cheeks and arms stung with zigzagged scratches. Pain banged behind my forehead, and right then nothing—not Smithers, not my parents, nothing—mattered more to me than putting my head down for a few minutes and closing my eyes.

Chapter
6

Something wakened me. It was well into morning, and the forest was still and strangely windless. The lichen on the old dead log where I had been lying irritated my sore cheek. I eased my left leg over the side, straddling the log like a horse, and pulled myself up to a sitting position.

It seemed much higher off the ground than it had in the half-light of dawn. Something wasn't right. A deep expectant silence filled the woods. I held my breath, listening for Smithers, but all I could hear was the trickle of the water in the creek below me.

A low rumbling vibration moved through the log. I knotted my fingers into the mossy bark and tightened my grip, sure the next sound I would hear would be the crisp shattering of timber cracking under me.

Instead, what came was a long, low, rolling rumble that worked its way up from deep in the earth and rose to the surface in a roar, like a thundering locomotive. A fierce shudder moved through the log and into me.

Then, with one swift heart-stopping jolt, the earth threw me and the log and the rest of the forest into chaos. The old tree took a deep lunge and nearly unloaded me. The whole world shook, as if it had been lifted by some giant hand, then rattled—the way my mother shook my jeans to empty the pockets. Hard. One. Two. Three good jerks.

Birds left the trees and filled the sky with screeching, shrieking clouds of movement.

For a moment, the quake faded. Then it came again, this time like a slow-motion movie, rolling like a boat on the ocean, dipping me and the log and the rest of the world on a crazy, sickening wave.

The trees that hung over the ravine swayed without wind. The brush jumped. Noise consumed me. Every kind of screaming, thundering, crying sound filled my ears and my head.

I flattened myself against the log and clung to it for dear life, praying to God to make it stop before I fell.

Then, just like that, it stopped. Stopped dead. As suddenly as it had come, it was over. And the world was quiet, still as a grave.

At first I was afraid to move. I had been in earthquakes before—you don't live in California all your life and not know about earthquakes. I had been through lots of them without ever being scared. The quake of '89, I had been outside playing with Deena when that one hit.

But this was different. This time I was alone, and I knew about aftershocks—if one came, there was no way I wanted to be stuck in midair on that wobbly log again.

To my right, a snag of greasewood was sticking out of the canyon wall. Without taking time to test its strength, I grabbed it and swung my right leg over the log and jumped off onto the embankment. As I landed, my sore ankle threw me off-balance, nearly sending me into the creek.

Dizzy and hungry, I ached all over. Worse, there was still no sign of Smithers.

"Smithers!" I screamed, and screamed again. If he didn't hear me, at least someone might. My voice sounded strange and vacant.

I had hated the quiet before the quake. I hated the noise when it came. But now, I hated even more the way the whole forest had already gotten back to normal. Everything—all the trees, the birds, the ground beneath me—was back in balance.

Everything except me. I still needed to catch up, reorganize, take account of what had happened. Things might seem the same, but they weren't. Now I was afraid, and I was alone. Not the good kind of alone I'd felt the day before, standing in the wind by myself at the river. This time what crept up inside me was an overpowering, desperate, cold kind of alone.

I was hardly in a safe place, stranded partway up a crumbling dirt bank with only a thin branch to hold on to. I thought about climbing down, or sliding on the seat of my pants, for that matter, but just then another rumble came from high up the ravine.

The noise was moving in my direction, growing louder. I knew it wasn't an aftershock. Leaning my body against the bank so I wouldn't tip backwards, I turned to see what it was. Heading toward me, tumbling, with the sound of snapping trees and moving earth, was a boulder, big as a truck.

My heart was thick in my throat. My breaths came fast and sharp. I tried to cry out, but nothing came.

Reaching over my head, I grabbed another branch. It cracked with my weight, but I held on and scrambled up the bank, out of the way of the huge white rock as it crashed down the canyon, tearing away the bank below me. With a loud roar, it splintered the log I'd slept on, rolled to the bottom of the creek, and plugged the canyon like a concrete dam.

When I'd gathered my wits, I found myself perched on an embankment high above the creek. Below me the ground broke into a sheer thirty-foot drop.

All morning I stood on that ledge wondering, wasn't anyone going to come for me? Could they be so mad at me for leaving that they were going to let me stay lost?

I couldn't call for Smithers anymore; my throat hurt too much, and I was too scared to even make myself cry.

But my fear was more than panic. It gripped me, confused me, made me want to scream and cry and jump at the same time. What Mom and Dad were going to do to me didn't matter anymore. I knew if I didn't do something soon, I'd be stuck there for the rest of my life.

I tested the shrubbery above me on the bank and pulled myself up, slowly spreading my body against the hill. Clods of dirt and rocks tumbled, showering the creek bed as I clawed my way to the top.

I came out in the trees on the edge of a small plateau, facing west toward the ocean and a lot higher than I'd expected. Ahead of me the hill sloped gently downward through the brush. If I went that way, I'd have a straight shot down to the river.

By the sun, I could tell it had to be close to noon. I knew Mom and Dad would be frantic, and I'd have a lot of explaining to do when I got back, especially since I hadn't even found Smithers for all my trouble. But with luck, I'd be home by lunchtime.

I checked my pocket. The arrowhead was still there. I took it out and stared at it for a moment. "It isn't luck, you know," my grandfather spoke inside my head. "It's all faith. The rock only reminds you to be strong. When you are, the rest will happen by itself."

Chapter
7

I forged downhill, battling twelve-foot greasewood bushes and walls of wild blackberries with my bare hands, shoveling myself into a thicket so high it blocked my view of the sky. All around, thorny branches reached for me. My face and arms were bloody with scratches. My jeans were torn, and I was beginning to wonder if I was even going in the right direction.

Then I saw daylight through an opening ahead. There was a break in the thicket, a meadow. Room to move.

But as soon as I stepped into the sunshine, I came to a dead stop. I had reached open air, but it was not a meadow. Where I had planned to cut a trail to the river—just where I was about to put my next step—the ground suddenly dropped away, in a wide gash. A massive chunk of earth had collapsed, just ripped off and sunk down into a steep, long brown V of mud, leaving my only route toward home a straight two-hundred-foot drop into the river.

Beside me, a huge Douglas fir teetered on the edge of

the cliff, leaning sideways, ready to drop. Other trees lay strewn haphazardly down the course of the slide, stuck sideways in the mud, like candles on a half-eaten piece of birthday cake.

The river seemed a lot different from the one I had waded across in the night. Sluggishly oozing like brown jam, it pushed around the mess of rocks and trees at the base of the cliff. From where I stood nothing looked familiar. Everything had changed. Even the way the light shone on the river was somehow different.

I kicked a large stone over the edge and watched it tumble down the slide and splash into the river. Although the water was directly below me, it was so far away I didn't hear the sound of the splash until the rock had disappeared into the water.

I yelled for help, over and over again. Each time, the wind blew my cry back at me.

The emptiness of my voice made me skittish, and I started to hear things I hadn't heard before, things inside my head, worries I knew I shouldn't listen to. And things outside my head, too, like silence—dead silence that sat over the valley like a vulture waiting for something to happen.

I don't know how long I sat there, with my knees bunched under my chin, trying to convince myself to take the first step down the cliff. But I couldn't move. I was so high up I began to feel sick, and just looking down made me sure I would fall if I tried.

Maybe if I waited there, Smithers might find me. Or maybe Mom and Dad would. Dad was too organized to let something like an earthquake mess up his plans. Yes, if I stayed put, everything would be fine.

Chapter
8

But it wasn't. The only thing that happened was that most of the day went by. Too soon, the sun fell toward the evening fog bank and long shadows began to stretch across the little clearing where I sat.

There'd been no sign of Smithers, no sign of my parents. I must have called for them a thousand times. But the shadows only got longer. My stomach hurt, my ankle pounded, and I was so thirsty that even the muddy river looked good enough to drink.

High above the hill on the other side of the river, an eagle circled in lazy spirals. Her lonesome cry, sounding as lost as I felt, floated to me. Like the fog that was drifting up the valley, fear crept back into me. I was getting cold.

I knew I shouldn't sit there all night long. Somehow, I had to find my way down to the river.

As I started toward the edge of the cliff, the eagle circled away from me, flying low over the valley in an elegant, gliding arc. She cried once more—but was it the eagle I heard? I waited for the sound to come again.

It was faint, far away, and this time coming from somewhere over the ridge in back of me. It hung in the air for only a second, then disappeared; but it was a warm, familiar sound. There was no mistaking it. What I was hearing was a dog's sad and lonesome howl. "Smithers!" I jumped to my feet, turned, and charged back through the brush.

When I broke out on the other side of the thicket, I waited at the spot where I'd climbed out of the canyon, thinking Smithers might still be down there. It seemed like hours passed as I waited to hear him again. When I finally did, his bark came from somewhere far over the hill on my right—nowhere near the canyon.

It didn't even cross my mind that I shouldn't go after him. Ducking beneath the branches of low-growing brush, I found a narrow, winding deer trail and followed it up the hill.

Soon the trees took over and the scrub brush gave way to the open floor of the forest, where it was dark and cool and I could run. My ankle hardly bothered me as I sprinted over fallen fir boughs, sheets of bark, and rotting wood. "Smithers!" I called as I ran.

The trail led me over the hill and down the other side. I'd never been in that part of the woods before. Between calls, I stopped to listen. Then I ran on. By the time I stopped to catch my breath, it was already twilight. High above me the stars were starting to appear. I held still and listened again. A breeze moved up the mountain, sweeping through the tops of the trees. Was something behind me? I spun around fast. Nothing. I began to run again.

I came out of the woods in a small clearing above the timber line, so high I could turn in a circle and look out over the whole darkening forest.

The length of the valley was spread before me, but I was all turned around. I couldn't make out any familiar landmarks. No smoke trails from campfires or chimneys, no smog from the city, no sign of the river anywhere. From where I stood, all the hills looked the same, stacked black, one against the other on the horizon for as far as I could see. I listened for Smithers, but the world was quiet. Only a lone eagle circled above me, too high for me to hear.

***

I don't know how much sleep I got that night. All I remembered about it when I woke up at dawn was that it had been too long and I'd been too cold—colder than I'd ever been in my life.

I heard barking again sometime around sunup. It was still ahead of me and seemed closer. But I was more lost than ever. And far past hunger. The farther I went, the more confused I got. Every tree began to look the same. Every turn familiar. By noon, only the gnawing pain in my belly moved me forward.

I looked for berries because that's what people eat when they get lost in the woods, but all I found were a few knobby red balls sprouting out on some broad-leafed bushes. I thought they might be thimbleberries, but I wasn't sure. When I tried to pick one, it squished like blood all over my hand, but I ate it anyway. And I snatched all the others, too.

I started thinking about Robinson Crusoe and his twenty-eight-year stay on that Caribbean desert island, and I remembered the book I'd read in sixth grade about the kid who got lost in the Canadian wilderness after a plane crash. That boy had seemed so real when I read about him, a tough kid who made it alone when everyone else thought he was dead.

But as I climbed on, I knew he was made up. At least he wasn't anyone I knew. Some writer could imagine a smart kid who figured things out, lived through horrible disasters, and saved himself from hopeless predicaments, but that was fiction. Right then, I was sure in real life things never worked out that way.

There had been lots of times in my life I'd wished I were alone, wished I didn't have to follow other people's rules. I was sure I'd be okay, like one of those street kids, tough and self-reliant. Just give me the chance. But now on the mountain, when I was really alone for the first time in my life, all I wished for was that there would be someone around to tell me what to do.

Chapter
9

I wanted to sleep, just rest my head on the warm grass and close my eyes. But I was too hungry to relax. Instead, I spread out on my back and stared up into the sky.

A patch of high clouds passed slowly overhead, a red-tailed hawk whistled, the sweet honey-yellow grass tickled the back of my neck. If I could have forgotten about what was really happening, it would have been a perfect day. I could almost imagine Papa D lying beside me, watching the sky for eagles.

I remembered telling him once that I thought the eagles were so handsome and free that if I got a second chance at living, I wanted to come back as one.

When I said that, Papa D shook his head and almost laughed at me. "An eagle only seems to be free," he said, raising his broad hand toward the sky. "That poor old bird's got a bond to nature that won't let her make a choice. If this were winter or early spring, she'd take whatever meal was easiest—probably a newborn lamb, unsteady on its feet and too far away from its mother. And an eagle hasn't a clue that when she takes a lamb, she takes the chance of ending up at the wrong end of a ranch hand's gun."

Papa D grumbled and sat up then, patting his chest with authority. "If I dare dream of coming back here after I pass on," he said with a chuckle, "I'd want to make sure I come back as a human being every time. We consider our choices, make our own decisions. And by the time we're grown, we usually know what will happen if we make a mistake."

As I recalled Papa D's words, a chill ran through me. I'd made so many mistakes already. I knew how getting lost in the woods usually turned out. You died of exposure, or thirst, or ended up bear food with no one finding you until your bones were lying brittle in the sun.

***

I wakened with a start, sure I was being watched. On my right, the brush stirred. Footsteps.

"Smithers?" I called weakly.

The late afternoon sun poked straight into my eyes so I couldn't see past my little circle of grass, but something told me what was coming toward me wasn't Smithers. I stood up, too weak to run, as a shadowy figure moved at the edge of the clearing.

Two men on horseback rode out from the cover of the trees. Three, no, four dogs trailed behind them. "Smithers!" I stumbled forward.

But none of the dogs was Smithers. They were all lean, and nervous, and they answered me with low suspicious growls.

"What do we have here?" One of the men hooted as he

pulled his chestnut mare to a stop and looked down at me. He had sandy hair, piercing blue eyes, and the broadest shoulders I'd ever seen.

I felt so small and overwhelmed it took me a few seconds before I realized that the man talking to me was Jack Matheson. I'd met him with Papa D the summer before, when we'd crossed paths at the river. Feebly, I began to introduce myself.

But Jack didn't seem to be listening to me as he climbed down and stood next to his horse. For someone who had seemed so huge the moment before, he was surprisingly short and boxlike beside me on the ground.

Without another word, he untied the canteen from his saddle and offered it to me. "You're Jim Abelard's boy, Rudy, aren't you?"

I nodded but couldn't speak as I put the water to my lips.

"Take it easy there, son. Don't gulp it all at once, or you'll founder." But I couldn't help it. It seemed no amount of water would ever quench my thirst.

As I handed the empty canteen back to him, the dogs closed in to sniff around my feet, and the other man rode out into the sunlight. I didn't recognize him but guessed he was the partner that my dad had mentioned.

"What the devil are you doing way out here in the woods?" the man said as he reined up beside Jack. He had a tooth missing on the right side of his mouth. It made a whistling sound when he spoke.

At first glance, I thought he was an old man. But as he rode closer, I saw that his face only seemed used up, like a piece of tarp left out in the sun too long.

Mirrored sunglasses shaded the man's eyes, but I could tell he was studying me. He bent over his saddle to get a closer look. "You lost or something, kid?"

"Have you seen my dog?" I stammered, not eager to admit I'd gotten lost. "He's just a pup. . . ."

The man shifted his weight in the saddle. "You say you're out here chasing after a dog?"

"He ran off yesterday, before the earthquake."

There was something unsteady about the man that made me not want to let him know too much. He looked at me so hard I had to turn away.

Jack moved between us. "Looks as if at least one of you got lucky," he said. "Out here, most times if someone takes off on his own, he ends up buzzard food, don't he, Sage?"

The other man didn't bother to answer but sat staring at me while he tapped his finger on the horn of his saddle.

"How long did you say you've been out here?" Jack said.

"I think it was yesterday. He ran off the night before the earthquake. Smithers . . . he's a yellow lab. Have you seen him? I heard him howling. . . ."

Jack broke into a chuckle and pointed to his dogs. "You can count on these old critters here to set to howling when they're on a trail. You gave them quite a run."

"You mean it was them I heard? All this time I've been thinking. . . . " I could feel my chest tightening, ready to give in to tears.

"Now, now, boy. Don't go getting all upset. Usually if a dog disappears in these parts, you never see him again. Bears get them. Sometimes sheep ranchers. But just so happens my nephew found a stray back of the house last night. . . ."

"You mean you found him? You have Smithers?"

"Back at the house. Friendly thing, isn't he? Kids took to him right away."

"Is he okay? He's not hurt or anything, is he?"

"Heck, no. He's in fine shape, better than you from what I can see. Tell you what. Let's fetch your dog and

48

get you something to eat. You look nearly as hungry as he did when he showed up."

I had forgotten about being hungry. Just hearing that they had Smithers made things all right. Relief wasn't a big enough word for the way I felt.

I wanted to ask a hundred questions: about Smithers, about my parents, about the earthquake. But neither of the men seemed to be the sort who'd want to answer. The man called Sage was stiff and unsmiling, and Jack was almost businesslike as he gave me an arm-up onto the back of his horse. I settled behind him, resting my leg against his rifle case.

Sage loped up beside us. "You sure you didn't run away?"

"No, sir. I was only looking for my dog."

He lowered his glasses and peered at me. "You said he took off into the woods. Was he after something?"

"I don't know. I guess so."

"Well . . . did you see anything or not? Bear, big cat, coyote?"

"No, I didn't see anything. It was dark. He was just running. . . ."

"Give it up, Sage," muttered Jack. "Can't you see the boy's exhausted?"

Jack whistled for the dogs, then kicked the horse forward, and I grabbed hold of the back of the saddle. "We're about four miles from home as the crow flies. Hang on tight."

We rode up through the trees, following the dogs and Sage as they trotted ahead. Knowing I was going to see Smithers soon made me feel I was almost home, and it crossed my mind that maybe there was such a thing as good luck after all.

Chapter
10

The four dogs kept up with the horses, tagging along like sidecars. Whenever one of them began to stray, Jack whistled and it quickly circled around, falling in at our heels. I decided they must be hounds. They weren't anything like Smithers. Those dogs seemed to have been born obedient.

We wound back and forth through the brush for ages, over and around fallen logs, down gullies and up again. It was slow going, and the hot sun on my back made me sleepy. Jack must have sensed it, because as my eyes began to close, he turned and said, "Rest your head if you like—it's a ways yet."

So I leaned against his back, not shy at all because I was so tired. He smelled comfortable, like smoke and laundry soap, and it eased me right off into a nap.

When I lifted my head, it was already near sunset. Only the tops of the trees were left in full light. The dogs were still padding along next to us, their tongues lolling sideways out of their mouths.

Jack reached around to hang onto me as we galloped up a steep grade. At the top, we came out of the brush onto a dirt road. It was a welcome sight. I hadn't seen a road in more than two days.

Suddenly Jack gave a long, low whistle. The hounds sped up. Noses to the dirt, they skirted past Sage, low murmurs rising from their throats. He slapped his horse on the rump, and pretty soon they were all running, disappearing around the bend in front of us, their howls swinging like a battle cry through the trees.

"Are they after something?" I asked, leaning around Jack's wide shoulder.

"No. They just smell home. I like to let them run the last mile. Gets their blood up, you know."

No, I didn't know. And right then I didn't care about anything except that "home" meant Smithers and a way to get back to my mom and dad.

***

As we came out of the trees, the road became only a path of tire tracks through the grass. Jack's mare clip-clopped at an eager stride, bouncing me behind the saddle.

"Whoa, girl!" he said, slowing the horse to a walk. Up ahead, a gate had been left open. It swung back and forth in the wind, banging against the fence post. Jack leaned over in the saddle and latched it behind us.

We rode through a dry, grassless field fenced by posts that looked as old as gravestone. A few mangy sheep moved away from us and huddled in a hot, dusty corner of the corral.

We kept going, through another gate, then past a series of sheds and a graying barn that stretched beneath a huge old pepperwood tree. It wasn't one of those homey-looking barns you see on the side of the highway surrounded by shiny pickup trucks and lots of dairy cows. Parts of the Matheson barn looked as though they were about to cave in.

I could hear a dog barking from inside the dilapidated old building. "Smithers?" I asked, nearly sliding off the horse in midstride.

"No, son. That's one of the mama hounds. Jezebel's her name. We keep her locked up in the shearing shed so she doesn't follow us when we ride off. She's got pups that need nursing. I believe your dog is up at the house." I heard Jezebel jump against the side of the shed. She continued barking as we passed.

From a distance, the house seemed huge. It was old-fashioned, three stories high, and square—the kind of house you see in western movies, with horses tied out front, firewood stacked to the side, and old men spitting tobacco over the porch rail. I leaned around Jack again to get a better look.

It seemed as if the house might have been nice at one time, about a thousand years ago, when it got its last paint job. Now it was a sickly, faded yellow, and it sagged with age. I could almost hear the paint peeling under the late afternoon sun.

Chickens and ducks squawked and scattered every which way as we crossed the dusty yard. Jack began to talk softly to his horse, patting her neck and reassuring her as we rode by a big white satellite dish lying on its side in the dirt.

"Damn thing spooks her every time." He shook his head. "Just bought that contraption last week. Quake dumped it over before we even got it mounted and plugged in."

It didn't look out of place with the stray tools and stacks of lumber scattered along the path between the barn and the house. Rusted cars, some without wheels, lay parked here and there around the yard, like so many tossed-out beer cans. The only thing that seemed to be in one piece was a blue sports car parked in a shed beside the house.

Smithers greeted me with an excited whimper before I even noticed him. He was tied to the front porch with a chain looped through his collar. A small boy, ragged and homely as a scrub mop, was sitting beside him on the top step. "Smithers!" I waved as Jack kicked us to a trot.

I was off the horse before Jack had time to rein her to a stop, my arms aching to hold Smithers. His wet tongue on my face helped hide the fact I was ready to cry.

"Seems to be your dog, all right." Jack laughed, easing himself to the ground.

Barefoot and shirtless, the boy sitting on the step was so occupied connecting dots on a piece of paper that he hardly looked up until Jack spoke directly to him.

"Squint, go inside and get your Aunt Colleen. Tell her to set another place at the table. Looks like we'll have company for at least one night." Jack turned to me then, resting his hand on my shoulder. "You don't mind staying over, do you, Rudy? It's too late to ride back across the river. It'll be dark soon, and I don't trust the roads at night, not since the earthquake."

A woman opened the screen door and came out onto the front porch holding a dripping paintbrush in her hand. She was tall, dressed in tight jeans and a yellow tank top with a dish towel tying back her black hair.

"What do you have there, Jack?" She grinned, coming down the stairs with her free hand outstretched. "Aren't we just crazy with strays these days?"

"Rudy, my wife, Colleen." He nodded as the woman shook my hand firmly. "The bookworm is my nephew. He's nine. Name's Duncan, but we call him Squint."

I could tell why when he peered up at me blinking through red hair that was snipped over his eyes.

54

"See what I made?" he said, holding up the paper so I could see the picture he'd drawn. "It's dot-to-dots. Not the store kind, I make them by myself." Even up close he was small for nine. I tried to remember my manners and say how nice I thought it was, but right then food was the only hospitality I was interested in.

"Colleen, do we eat soon? Rudy hasn't had a meal since before the earthquake."

"It's almost ready," she said, holding the door open for me with her elbow. We were all wondering, Jack, where you and Sage were. We expected you back this morning."

"Quake brought down lines all over the place. Phone's not going to work for days as far as I can tell. Good thing we've got the generator because it'll take weeks before we get our electricity running steady."

"Never mind. We can do without. I'm just grateful we're all safe." The screen hissed closed behind her.

Jack's boot heels clicked across the old plank floor, but my sneakers didn't make any sound at all. It made me feel awkward and out of place, as if I was intruding.

As Colleen led us into the front room, Jack told her how they had found me. "Don't feel bad. We'll get you home real soon. What you need now is a bath and something to eat. But you'll have to forgive the mess, Rudy. That shaker took nearly everything out of my cupboards and threw it across the room. I'm still mopping up."

But I loved the room. It was cheerful and sort of untidy, with stacks of newspapers and paperback books lined against the walls. It reminded me a little of my grandmother's parlor, the one in Papa D's old house in Stockton. Like that room, it was wrapped waist-high in dark polished wood.

I remember Papa D used to polish the wainscot in the Stockton house, even after Grandma died. I guess some old men shine their cars or clean their pipes, but my grandfather used to polish the woodwork in that old house until the whole place smelled like a lemon orchard.

Colleen set a sandwich on the table, and it almost gagged me to swallow. I guess sometimes you can be too hungry to eat, like being too tired to sleep. She turned to face Jack. "Did you feel any of the aftershocks? I lost Mother's best serving platter this morning." She sighed but didn't finish, straightening herself proudly as she grinned down at me. "From now on, till the earth quits shaking, I'm sticking to paper plates."

Jack turned to me. "I'll get Squint to help me set up a cot in his room," he said. "He snores, hope you don't mind. When you take your bath, toss your clothes in the hamper by the tub, and Colleen will wash out the ticks. I'll scout around for a pair of pants and a shirt you can borrow till they're dry. Just make sure you empty the pockets first. She's got a thing about forgetting to do that."

I followed Colleen down the hallway, past what might have once been the parlor, and up a wide staircase to a landing where a tall window faced out onto the darkening yard. The air on the second floor was heavy and musty, holding the heat of the day like Papa D's attic used to do in the summertime.

Colleen pointed to the bathroom. "Towels are in the cupboard over the tub. Take as long as you want."

I locked the door behind me. There was no way I was going to strip down past my underwear in a strange bathroom unless I could lock the door. I wished I could just pretend to bathe, but running the water and swooshing it around like I sometimes used to do at home wouldn't work this time. My arms were scratched. My ankle was scraped. In the mirror I could see dirt cemented in the wide crease on my forehead, spiraling into the circle of my ear. I was as filthy as I had ever been—even my eyelids were dirty.

I emptied my pockets, setting my arrowhead and the picture of Papa D on the table by the sink. Then I undressed fast and hopped into the tub, feeling exposed, sort of the way I had when I was alone in the woods.

When I was back downstairs, Jack took the head of the table. Colleen sat at the other end. Sage sauntered over to the coat rack, hung up his jacket, and took a gun out of his belt. Then he pulled out a chair and parked himself beside Squint.

As he sat down, he lay the gun at the top of his table setting in front of the plate, posting it crosswise next to his water glass as if it was just another piece of silverware, like a fork or a spoon. Its barrel was silver-black. I had never seen a real hand gun unholstered before, and my mouth must have been hanging open in amazement. But no one else took a second look.

Colleen placed cold roast beef and chicken in front of me. That was followed by a basket of bread and a pitcher of milk. As she filled my plate, she explained proudly that all the vegetables were from Jack's garden out back.

From the time he had sat down, Sage had been studying me, his whisker-stubbed chin twitching up and down as he chewed. Squint had his eyes square on me, too, and although he was smiling, I was sure both he and Sage thought I was a fool for getting lost the way I did.

Halfway through the meal, the door swung open and a tall blonde girl blew into the room. She looked about fifteen or sixteen, and she didn't even notice me as she hooked her hat on the peg behind the door and leaned over to take off her boots.

"Rudy," said Colleen, a tone of apology in her voice, "I'd like you to meet Circe MacLeod, my niece. Circe is Squint's sister."

Circe . . . ? It sounded like a name you'd give to a candy bar. Turning, she nodded in my direction. On a closer look, I could see I'd been wrong. From the expression on her face, this girl didn't seem to have any sweetness about her. She looked as bitter as acorns as she tossed her boots into the corner and marched over to join us at the table. It was none of my business, but I could feel anger sparking the air.

Colleen glared at the girl as if she was expecting trouble. I had to concentrate on my vegetables to keep from staring at her.

Jack set his fork down slowly. "And why are you so late, young lady? Don't you want any supper tonight?"

"I was doctoring TomDog is all," Circe snapped, pushing her hair off her forehead. It was short, cut square above her ears the way Squint's was over his eyes, but long on one side. That made bangs she had to toss off her face every few seconds.

Jack's fork went down to his plate again. "I'll give you only one more day. I knew I should have put him down when he first got sick. No one needs a damn incontinent dog. Animal like that is no good to anyone."

"Now, Jack." Colleen's voice was calm, but she continued to glare at Circe. "Maybe with her care—"

"No. It isn't right to let him limp along barely hanging on to life the way he is. He's past his time and, mind me, Circe, I'm drawing the line on tomorrow night. If he doesn't improve a whole lot by then, I'm taking over, no matter what Colleen and all the rest of you bleeding hearts say. He's my dog, and I'm going to damn well be the one to decide what'll happen to him."

Abruptly, Sage shoved back his chair and stood up, retrieving his gun. No one said a word as he snatched the leftover chicken leg off his plate, pulled his wind-breaker from the hook, and went out the door. It crossed my mind that maybe he was going to go out and shoot poor TomDog right then.

Beside me, Circe was quiet, building a little pyramid of peas in the middle of her plate. Just like that, she had lost her fire, a different person than the one who stomped in the door a few minutes ago. Right then she looked as if she might be about to cry.

Jack sliced another piece of roast and slapped it onto his plate. "Child, you know that's the way it has to be. There's no use sniveling about it now."

For such a short man, Jack Matheson sure seemed to take up a lot of space.

Chapter
11

The high ceiling and bare floor bounced the sounds in the kitchen back and forth, louder than normal—sounds I guess I had never noticed much at home. The clicking of silverware as Colleen opened a drawer, a chair sliding over the floor, a pot set on the drainboard. All at once I was full of emptiness, there in that houseful of strangers.

Jack must have sensed I was uneasy. "Guess you've figured out that we've got a bit of a problem with our phones. I'm real sorry, but you won't be able to let your folks know you're all right." He stepped up beside me and gave me a pat on the back. "Tell you what. You get a good night's sleep and I'll drive you to town first thing in the morning, then we'll look up the sheriff. Your mom and dad have probably already contacted him."

I nodded. It seemed I had no choice.

Circe carried an armload of dishes into the kitchen. "So what is someone like you doing way out here in Neverland?" she asked as she scraped leftovers into a bucket beside the sink. "You look like a city kid to me."

Funny, I thought, I would have pegged her for a city person, too. She seemed hard for a country girl, and up close I saw her ear was pierced in three places.

"We have a campsite," I started to explain. "Down at the river. I was with my parents. . . . Then I guess I got lost."

"You're lucky Jack found you. It usually takes a guardian angel to get a person out of these woods once they dig in this far." She scooped up the last puddle of gravy and dropped it into the bucket. "As long as you're here, you might as well make yourself useful and give me a hand."

"Are you feeding Smithers, too?" I asked.

She smiled, tossing the hair off her forehead. "So, that's his name. Sure, I'm feeding him. Uncle Jack puts him into the shearing shed with the other dogs for the night, but he doesn't seem to mind. He's a sweet pup. How'd you manage to get separated from him?"

"It was the middle of the night. He ran off, and I went after him. He's young. I guess he didn't know any better."

"Kind of like you?" She laughed and handed me the bucket of scraps. "We misplace hounds sometimes, when they're running a bear or a mountain lion. Occasionally the young ones get lost. If they come back, Jack usually shoots them for being stupid."

That didn't make much sense to me. "If they're smart enough to find their way home, why would he shoot them?"

"Because they were dumb enough to get lost in the first place. It means they're not like other hounds. They're defective, kind of like my brother." She turned her head so no one would hear, then whispered, "Squint's backward. You'll see. He's strange about some things." With that, she was headed for the door. I grabbed the screen before it slammed in my face and followed her onto the porch.

Evening sounds had begun to fill up the shadowy spaces around the yard. Behind the barn where the moon was rising, the forest rimmed the hills, spiny and black. I walked close to Circe, careful not to let the bucket slosh against my leg.

"Do you and Squint stay here all summer?" I asked, trying to keep up with her as we followed the road past the barn. She didn't answer me until we reached the pens by the shearing shed where the dogs were kept.

"No," she said, then lifted the latch on the door and stepped inside. "This is where we live."

The dogs began to kick up a fuss as soon as Circe unlocked the gate on the pen. "Pour that stuff into the big pan," she told me, opening a metal garbage can and scooping dry food into the scraps. "Stir them together. I'll get the dishes. You'd better not get too close to the dogs. They don't take to strangers much better than anyone else around here."

Jezebel, the mother dog, snarled as we passed her pen. "Jezzie is Jack's best work dog. She usually has free run of the place, but now he has to shut her up when he goes out riding. She's got four pups. She had seven, but three died because at first she wouldn't stick around to let them nurse. We had to lock her in there with them. Now she won't let any of us near."

Smithers was separated from the other dogs by a gate of wire mesh, and he jumped up happily when I let myself into his pen.

"He's a real nice dog," Circe said as she filled Smithers's water dish. "But he'd be nicer if he had some manners."

I knelt beside him in the hay and watched him eat. Every few moments he stopped and turned his head, checking to make sure I was still there. "I guess the way he runs off, I can't blame your uncle for keeping him tied to the porch."

"Oh, it isn't Uncle Jack that keeps him tied," Circe said as she retrieved the bucket. "It's Sage. He's real nervous about dogs running loose around here. Uncle Jack used to let the dogs run free all the time before Sage came. Now every one of them is penned as soon as the sun goes down."

I wanted to ask more, but before Smithers had finished, Circe motioned to me that we'd better get back. "I have other chores to do," she said.

As we passed back along the hounds' pens, I asked her which one was TomDog.

"He isn't here. I have him shut up in one of the lambing pens."

"How come? Is he dangerous?" One of the dogs growled, eying me cautiously as it circled its dish.

"Heck, no. He's as gentle as a puppy, you'll see—if you get the chance. He's just too sick to be with the other dogs. They worry and fuss over him too much."

"What's the matter with him?"

"He's just old." Circe closed the gate behind me and we left the shed.

As we crossed the yard toward the house, I noticed Sage, only a dim figure in the shadow of the porch. The light from his cigarette colored his face every moment or so. I had the feeling he was watching us, but before we reached the front walk, he squashed his cigarette with his boot heel and went back inside.

"Is being old the only thing wrong with TomDog?"

"Yes," Circe said, scuffing her feet in the dust. "But around here, that's enough."

Upstairs, the light had been left on by the cot where I was supposed to sleep. The bed was small, but tucked cozily under the window. Across the room, Squint's covers were folded back neatly. A stuffed brown rabbit waited for him on his pillow.

A pencil and pad lay on the table by his bed. I couldn't see what was on it, but guessed it was another dot-to-dot project, like the one he'd been working on when I arrived.

I was just about to lie down when he came into the room. His slippers scuffed over the wooden floor. He had something in his hand.

"You left these in the bathroom," he said, approaching my cot. "It's a real nice arrowhead. I've never seen one like it before." He came up beside me, holding on tightly to my arrowhead and the picture of me and Papa D. "Is it your good luck charm?" he asked as he handed it to me.

"Sort of," I said, knowing that Papa D always insisted I shouldn't think of it as lucky, that it was only "a piece of faith," as he called it. "A piece of faith," he'd say and look into my eyes hard, the way he did when he wanted me to keep something in my head forever. "But you'll never see the real wonder of it till the day you have strength enough to give it away."

"My grandfather gave me the arrowhead," I said, looking back up at Squint. "He found it somewhere down by the river."

Squint shuffled his slippers back and forth over the floor, still holding onto the photograph. "Who's in the picture?" he asked shyly.

"That's me, last year. And my grandfather." I reached for it, but Squint backed away.

"Don't be mad," he said. "I didn't do it." He hesitated, then put it into my hand.

I hadn't noticed when I emptied my pants, but as he handed it to me, I saw that my picture was bent in half and crumpled around the edges. Now Papa D and I were separated into two pieces. On the left side I was still smiling, but a deep jagged crease began at my feet and sliced diagonally up to my knee, then over the red-and-black plaid of Papa D's shirt before it ripped across his face, puckering the picture in half above his left eye.

"I didn't do it. Honest, I didn't. It was like that. . . ."

"That's okay," I lied. "It must have happened before I took it out of my pocket. It was in there a long time."

Squint seemed satisfied, and without any more conversation shuffled to his bed, tucked himself under the covers, and reached for his pad and pencil. Seconds later, he was busily drawing as if I wasn't even there.

The picture in my hand felt like an insult staring back at me; the only picture I had of Papa D, the one I wanted to remember him by, had been ruined by my own carelessness.

Little flecks of the photo were already peeling off the paper around the crease on Papa D's face. They reminded me of the old coat of paint chipping off the outside of the Matheson house. I wanted to fix it, smooth it out, and make it the way it was before. It would have worked if I pressed the flat part of my fingernail on the crease and rubbed a little, but all at once, touching Papa D's ruined face seemed too real. I was afraid if I messed with it I would make it worse. Some part of me didn't want to be that close to him—so close I might do more harm.

I pulled the covers around my chin and waited for sleep, staring up at the ceiling, thinking about Smithers out there alone in the barn and about Papa D alone in his room at the hospital. A breeze flickered at the shutter, knocking it gently against the side of the house. A pair of footsteps faded down the hall. A door closed.

As I lay there in the dark, I realized for the first time that I was more lonesome in that houseful of people than I had been when I was alone on the mountain the night before.

Chapter
12

In the morning, I wakened to an empty room. Squint's bed was already made, and the clothes he'd thrown on the chair the night before were gone. I sat up, listening for voices from the kitchen below. Had Jack forgotten he was going to take me to town?

I pulled on my sneakers without tying them, this time leaving the photo but making sure I had my arrowhead with me.

When I got downstairs, the kitchen was empty, too. I realized I was the last one up.

Smithers pawed at the screen door when he saw me. He was tied up again, but had plenty of slack to move around.

Out back of the house, an argument was going on. I untied Smithers and walked slowly around the corner of the porch.

It was Sage. He was standing by the clothesline, shaking his fist at Colleen.

"What's the matter with the fool thing now?" he said

tightly. "I thought Jack fixed the fuel pump."

Colleen took the clothespin out of her mouth and clipped it onto my jeans on the line. "It's the carburetor again." Her voice was calm, but I felt her impatience. "He says he'll have it put together by tomorrow morning. Don't worry."

Sage turned away from Colleen and saw me. I had a sudden urge to take a quick duck behind the corner but held my ground. There was no use hiding. He'd spotted me already and was heading my way.

"Can't we take him out in the car?" he said, gesturing toward the shed where the sports car was parked. As he extended his arm, I noticed a row of deep scratches running between his wrist and his elbow.

"No. I told Jack I didn't want anyone trying to get my car around any mud slides or through any ditches. The earthquake might have brought down almost anything. The car stays put until somebody checks out the road."

Sage's eyes settled on me. "Guess he's not going home today then, is he?"

Colleen saw me then, too, and she left Sage and the laundry. "I'm sorry, Rudy. It can't be helped. You don't mind staying one more day, do you?"

I shook my head, my throat too tight to bring out any words. Smithers nudged my leg.

"Well, mind me, son." Sage pointed a bony finger at Smithers. "You leave that animal of yours tied up. Don't let me find him wandering off. I won't be responsible for what happens to him if—"

"Sage! Don't be hard on the boy. He's only visiting, and that dog's as friendly as your own mama." She leaned to pat Smithers, his tail thumping up and down in the dust. "Sage is right, though. You will have to keep track of him. Let's tie him back up on the porch while you have breakfast."

Jack came up the walk while I was tying Smithers. "I

suppose Colleen told you the bad news. Hope you aren't too disappointed about not going home today. Your folks must be real worried about you by now."

"It's okay," I said, guiding Smithers to the dish of water by the door. "Everyone's been real nice. I hope we're not too much trouble."

"Not a chance." Jack laughed and gave Smithers a scratch. "Good dog you've got here. He'd make a great tracker with a little training."

When we got back inside, Sage was already eating, a napkin stuffed beneath his chin, his gun in the same position it had been in the night before. He tapped his fingers on the table.

Jack sat down opposite Sage at the table. "We had another kill last night," he said, a tone of disgust in his voice. "I tell you, we're going to lose more sheep than ever this season if that government hunter doesn't hustle up and get out here."

"It wasn't a lion, was it?" Colleen asked anxiously.

"No, not this time. Single kill, not much left." Jack smeared a glob of butter over his stack of pancakes and swigged syrup over them. "No evidence of bear, either. It was likely a coyote."

Sage pushed away from the table, stood, and hitched up his pants. "Could be a stray dog passing through." He nodded in my direction. "Like other visitors of the day that are out of their home range, it might already know it's roaming off course where it shouldn't be." He pulled his sunglasses from his breast pocket and left the room, his boots thumping hard down the steps outside.

"Sage must have indigestion." Jack laughed. "Don't mind him. He gets like that sometimes."

Colleen passed the milk to me. "Circe hasn't come down yet. She was up half the night with that old dog. She's fallen in love with him. I don't imagine she'll sleep much longer, though. Squint's been up for hours. Probably out in the shearing shed or off in the hills some-where. I'm afraid you won't see him till lunchtime, Rudy.

"Why don't you leave Smithers on the porch and go with Jack? He has to set the water lines in the garden before the sun's too high. It will give you a chance to see his pride and joy."

I followed Jack out the door, down the steps, and over the narrow dirt path at the side of the house. He took long strides in front of me, walking sort of like my dad, purposefully, at an evenly measured pace.

The garden was protected by a high fence, with barbed wire strung along the top. "I don't usually allow the children in here," Jack said as he stooped to flip the latch on the gate.

The garden seemed as if it belonged to a different world from the rest of the ranch. It was huge, and laid out in neatly labeled rows of vegetables: squash, cucum-bers, peas, carrots, lettuce, beans, and cornstalks were lined up one after the other in rows as perfect as tailors' seams.

I must have been looking stupidly surprised because Jack smiled and leaned toward me. "Come on. Don't tell me you've never seen a garden before."

"Not one like this," I stammered, trying not to be rude in my amazement. "Are those berries over there?"

"I've got blackberries, both Himalayan and wild, raspberries, loganberries, and over there, under the bird netting, some strawberries. I get lots better odds in this garden than anywhere else on the ranch." He laughed. "Jays are a whole lot easier to keep out than coyotes."

I followed him as he crossed to another path leading to the rear of the garden. "I had to cut away a few trees to get the right sun exposure for these roses."

I didn't even have to get close to smell them. I had never seen so many roses, and in more colors than I'd ever imagined roses could be.

Just as I was thinking how my mother would have gone crazy over them, Jack asked, right out of the blue, "How's that granddad of yours? Haven't seen hide nor hair of him for ages."

My heart jumped. Quickly I looked away from Jack's friendly grin. I'd forgotten he knew Papa D. How was I going to tell Jack what had happened to him?

I was still searching for the words when Jack stopped in the path and stared down at one of the rosebushes, shaking his head. "Damn," he muttered. "Hand me those gloves over there on the post, will you, Rudy?"

I gave him the gloves, and he knelt to the ground, still shaking his head. "This one's lost its vigor. Just look at it. It's got no chance to thrive."

The small bush quivered, and apricot-colored petals showered his head and shoulders as he tugged at the stubborn root. "Spoils the looks of the whole garden to have one failing plant," he said, puffing from the effort. Jack kept on yanking the rosebush with one hand, digging around its base with the other. At last the whole plant tore out of the ground.

"Good man, your grandfather," he said, standing to wipe the sweat from his forehead. "Did he come up here with your family?"

"No, he didn't come this year," I answered, dropping my voice. "He . . . he had a stroke."

Jack stopped in the path and gazed back at me. I could tell he was stunned. "A stroke? Well, what do you know? I'm real sorry to hear that. He was such a wonderful man."

It was the times I wasn't thinking about Papa D at all that the shame of my secret wish that he was already dead sneaked up on me. I never let it come into my head on purpose. It only showed up when I had my guard down, like just then, as I followed Jack across the garden.

71

Part of me thought it would be easier if he was. That way I wouldn't have to think about him still looking like he did the last time I saw him, with his deep, blank eyes trying to follow my movements around the room.

But as I watched Jack toss the dying rosebush onto the compost heap at the edge of the garden, I knew that shame wasn't a word terrible enough for the way I felt.

Chapter
13

We left the garden, crossing the yard together as far as the barn, where two horses were saddled and waiting. Jack pointed to the house.

"Go on back now, and see if Circe's pulled herself out of bed yet. Not that it will do you any good. She'll probably spend most of the day with that damn dog again." He waved his arm toward the shearing shed. "She's got her brother all upset over him, too. . . . I could wring her neck! She ought to know an old dog like that isn't worth the shavings off a bald man's head." He left me then, shaking his head as he walked over to the horses.

I felt Sage come up behind me. "Didn't misplace your dog already, did you?" he mumbled, standing so close to me I could smell the tobacco on his breath.

He stepped around in front of me and reached inside his jacket the way a movie cop might go for his gun. But it wasn't his gun he was reaching for. Instead, he took out a little package of candy. Unfolding the foil wrapper, he popped a small purple square into his mouth.

"They're 'Violets'," he said, holding them out to me. "Want one?" They smelled like my grandmother's closet. I shook my head, and he shrugged, then moved off toward his horse.

"Sage and I will be spending most of the day riding fence and putting things back in order around here," said Jack as he climbed into his saddle. "As if it'll do any good. The earthquake caused a lot of damage. Don't know why I bother fixing anything around here anymore. Ranching's a lost way of life. Seems like we've got everything working against us these days." He paused, taking a long look at the hills, then the house and the barn. "You're welcome to explore. Just make sure you stay out of the barn. Damn quake did its work everywhere."

I watched Sage lean back on his horse and unwrap another candy. While he rolled the little piece of foil into a tiny ball between his fingers, he kept his eyes fixed on me. "If you take it into your mind to nose around this place, don't go past the gate at the fork in the road. And," he said, kicking his horse forward and pulling up so close to me I had to back up to avoid getting stepped on, "whatever you do, don't let that dog of yours out of your sight. Got that straight, kid?"

"Yes, sir." I nodded, wishing they'd just hurry and leave. Sage made me feel all wrong somehow, like Smithers and I were mistakes he couldn't wait to erase.

Jack rode up beside me. "Here, take this," he said, leaning over to hand me his wrist watch. "It's eleven now. Be back by two. And if you go as far as the fork in the road, like Sage said, stay on this side of the gate."

I glanced past the barn in the direction of the woods and saw Squint standing by the fence. I couldn't see his eyes in the shadows, but I knew he was staring hard at his uncle and me.

74

By the time I got back to the house, Circe was on the porch polishing her toenails. Smithers was lying beside her, so content he didn't lift his nose from his paws as I walked up. I stroked the soft, warm place behind his ears, and his tail flopped happily. Circe looked up from her toes as I sat down. "Hey there, Rudy. Staying out of trouble?"

Colleen came out of the house then and set her coffee mug on the railing. "I guess morning is the finest time of day in the summer." She sighed, stretching her arms over her head. "As far as I know, you can't beat a morning like this anywhere else on earth."

She sat beside me on the step, warming her hard, tanned hands on the cup. In the sunlight, her hair was so black it looked purple.

"I remember my mama saying that she couldn't stand the loneliness of this place," Colleen went on. "I guess that's why she and Papa didn't live here long. But even as a child I loved it, just the peace of it, the air, the quiet.

"Not like my sister. She's a city girl. . . . Can't stand dirt, you know. She's got to have a shower twice a day. Needs to sip white wine and wear high heels. Likes city noises, she says. Suppose some people think mine's a solitary life, but to me the city's a lot lonelier place to live."

A look passed between Colleen and Circe. The girl's eyes were suddenly as sharp and angry as they had been at dinner the night before.

"Ah," Colleen continued, shaking her head knowingly, her eyes still holding Circe. "Yes. Your mother is a different person now from the sister I knew. And what she's done to you children put her so far away from me I've never—"

Suddenly, the moment was broken. The porch dipped. The railing creaked. "Oh, Lord! It's another one!" Colleen jumped to her feet.

At the far end of the corral, Jack yanked his horse to a halt. Sage pivoted at the fence, and they both turned to look back at the barn, watching it quiver until the earthquake passed. The house gave one more little bump, and then it was over, before anyone had time to say another word.

But the dogs were going loony in the pens in the shearing shed, their barks turning to endless, anxious yapping.

"Damn barn'll be the next thing to go!" Jack hollered, reining his horse around. Colleen moaned and raced inside the house.

"I wish the aftershocks would stop," Circe said. "They make Colleen so jittery. She fluffs up like a nervous pigeon with each one, and for hours she tiptoes through the house rebracing her treasures as if she expects 'The Big One' to hit any minute."

"No damage this time," said Colleen as she returned to the porch and sat beside us. "But I'll feel safer with all of you outside today—in case a bigger one comes. Besides, I don't want you locking yourself up with that old dog again today, Circe. It's not healthy."

Circe continued working on her nails. After a moment she said, "Uncle Jack's going to put TomDog down, no matter what, isn't he, Auntie Coll?"

Colleen drew a deep breath. "You know he will, honey." She placed a hand on the girl's knee. "He won't waste worry over a dog that can't work. You're a strong girl. You know how these things have to be. I only hope Squint doesn't take it too hard. He's as sensitive as smooth water to a breath of wind. It seems he's got his heart too far into that old dog to let him go."

Circe capped the polish and stuck out her toes in the sun. She gazed toward the shearing shed and sighed. "Squint talks to TomDog a whole lot, you know. It gives me the creeps. He sits real close to him and tells him everything will be all right, but I don't think he really believes it."

"But you do, don't you, darlin'?" Colleen moved her arm up around Circe's shoulder.

It made me uncomfortable to overhear the problems of people I had known for such a short time. I felt as if I was a spectator sitting on the outside of a circle game and watching it take its course without being able to get inside, as if the world these people lived in was totally separate from mine, rolling around in front of me, coming close and almost bumping me but veering away before I could touch it. Not much about any of them made sense to me.

"TomDog's going to be fine," Circe said at last. "When I left him last night, he almost got up to follow me. He should be lots better by the end of the day. You'll see."

Colleen looked up and shaded her eyes, staring wistfully at the shed. "It would be so wonderful if he would, for everyone's sake. But I know in Jack's mind he's already dead, and it might be better for both of you to think of him that way, too. It's going to break hearts when he has to be put down." Colleen sighed and lifted the cup to her lips. She got up to go back inside, sipping carefully, as if the coffee were still hot.

Chapter
14

"I've packed a lunch for you," Colleen said, coming back out onto the porch. "You'd better finish up there, Circe. It seems Squint's taken to the hills again."

"You ought to make a rule that he can't go off the way he does," said Circe. "Then we wouldn't have to go to all this trouble."

"I wouldn't call his roaming trouble—tiresome maybe, but not trouble. If you like, Rudy can go along, too. There's lunch enough for both of you—and for Squint, when you find him."

"Where do we go to look for him?" I asked.

"Oh, back in the woods usually. Never very far. Circe pretends to look for him. It's kind of a game, I guess. He wanders off every other day or so. He's not lost, but he'll stay out until she goes to look for him."

"Like I told you last night," Circe said, peering down her nose at me, "my brother's backward."

"He isn't either." Colleen scowled. "Squint's an angel.

He's a real good boy. Never gets into a speck of mischief. Now don't be gone too long. If Jack thinks you're lost again, Rudy, he'll send the dogs out after you."

"Don't worry. He told me to be back by two. I have his watch." I held up my arm to show her. The watch flopped over and slid down to my elbow.

Circe took the lunch sack from Colleen. "Are you ready to play hide-and-seek with my nutty brother?"

"Can we take Smithers, or should we leave him tied?"

She grinned and scratched him on the head. "Does he have a nose for finding things?" Smithers wagged his tail. "Sure you do, don't you, boy? Come on. You'll be a big help."

A long silence followed us past the barn and up the road into the woods. When we spoke, it was at a whisper, more not to disturb the forest than to sneak up on Squint. The woods were so quiet that I was sure if Squint had been anywhere close by, he couldn't help hear us coming. Each one of our footsteps sent birds into the air.

Every once in a while Circe darted her head from side to side, eying the woods beyond the edge of the road. "It's so quiet, it feels like someone's watching, doesn't it?" she finally said.

I stopped in the road and looked behind me. Smithers was keeping up, still skipping in and out of the trees.

"There's nothing. If there was, Smithers would let us know." But I felt it, too—the same exposed feeling that had come on me when I was lost earlier.

"I know nothing's after me, but I get the jitters out here all the time. Squint says I'm silly. According to him, when you feel that way, it's your guardian angel following you."

"Do you ever find him?" I asked, glancing over my shoulder as casually as I could.

"When he first started playing the game, it was hard

for me to pretend not to find him. He'd be almost in plain sight. But now it really is hard. I never find him. Usually he finds me. Just when I think I've really lost him, he sort of appears from nowhere and gives me a hug. A little weird, huh?" Circe stepped closer to me and spoke at a whisper.

"Auntie Coll and Uncle Jack had to take him out of school in the middle of kindergarten because he wanted to hold the teacher's hand all the time. He wouldn't leave her alone. It's like he's got this need to be close and touching everything. Sometimes I think that's why he likes to play the game. The closeness gets to be too much, and he needs to get away, be separate from the rest of us for a while."

The light in the woods was shallow and twitched spookily at the trees. It was comforting to have Smithers along. He zigzagged from one side of the road to the other, sniffing the brush.

"How come your brother's like that?"

Circe hesitated. "They say it's because my mother never held him when he was a baby."

We walked on quietly for a while, scuffing along the dirt road and whistling for Squint now and then. I hoped he wasn't out there overhearing our conversation.

"It wasn't that she didn't love him," Circe said, absently staring up into the trees. "She worried more about him than she did about me. Mama was always afraid something was going to happen to him."

She slowed down for a moment and turned to me. "I remember watching her walk up to his crib when he was tiny and get real close, close enough to look over the side and see he was breathing, and she'd reach out to touch him. But then all of a sudden she'd back away, afraid almost, like she'd seen a monster lying there instead of a baby."

I didn't know what to say. We'd walked quite far, and

81

it was getting hot. Circe puffed and pushed the hair off her face. "I'm beat. Let's quit for a while and eat lunch." She untied the bandanna from around her neck. "I'm boiling, aren't you?"

She parked herself on a stump by the road. "Darn him anyway. I waste half my days running around in these trees looking for him." She peeled the plastic wrap off her sandwich. "Backward. There's no other way to say it."

"He wouldn't go past that gate your uncle told me about, would he?"

Circe tossed her hair out of her eyes and focused hard on me. The look she gave me was somewhere between surprise and laughter. "No, he'd never do that. Squint doesn't break rules." She took a deep swallow of her soda and let it go down slowly. "Colleen says he 'walks the straight and narrow' because he's afraid no one will love him if he disobeys. Besides, he might be backward, but he's not stupid. He knows he'll get skinned if he goes over there."

We went on eating our peanut-butter sandwiches and drinking warm soda without saying much more. The sun had broken through the trees and was beating down on top of us. I checked the watch. An hour and a half to go.

"Where's Smithers?" Circe asked, turning to look back down the road. "Don't tell me he's run off, too?"

I hadn't even noticed he was gone. But thinking about it, I knew if he was around he would have been right in front of me, begging for my lunch.

"I'll be back," I said, handing her my soda can. "Wait for me. He can't have gone very far." She nodded, then waved as I ran up the road.

Chapter
15

I caught a glimpse of him about a hundred yards down the road ahead of me, trotting along without a care in the world, his tail pointing high in the air.

He must have heard me coming, but he didn't stop or slow down. He simply turned and glanced slyly back at me, then ran on.

Smithers was fast for a young dog. At least he seemed to always be fast when I was after him, and as I picked up speed, so did he, running on just so I would chase him. It was his favorite game.

I told myself to be grateful that at least this time he was sticking to the road and not leading me into the woods. But as I followed him around a turn, all at once the forbidden gate lay across the road in front of me. Trespass at Risk! stood out on a sign in boldly painted red letters.

I knew from Papa D that on this side of the river those words always meant exactly what they said. I remembered Sage's cold gray gun stationed like a warning flag on the dinner table, and I slowed to a walk.

Smithers stopped to sniff around the gatepost.

"Here, boy," I said, as calmly as I could, praying the sound of my voice wouldn't make him bolt again.

Smithers raised his head and glanced over his shoulder, almost smiling at me. I took a step toward him. With a sudden burst of speed, he skinnied himself down flat and shimmied under the gate.

I whistled, but by the time I reached the gate, he was already on his way up the hill on the other side. And he was going at a full gallop, not even bothering to look back at me.

All the eyes of the forest seemed to focus on me as I began to climb the gate. The only sound was the creak of the old boards under my weight. I wanted to whistle for Smithers, but my mouth was too dry.

For some crazy reason, as I swung my leg over the top rail, a picture of my dad came into my head. He was decked out in his clean socks and hiking shorts, guidebook in one hand, binoculars in the other. Raising the glasses, he checked out the road, then shook his head. "Nothing there," his phantom voice said to me. "Give it up before you get in trouble."

Trouble? What trouble? No one was going to catch me. Besides, there wasn't time to worry about being caught—I couldn't even see Smithers anymore. He'd already disappeared around the bend on the other side of the gate.

I jumped down to the ground and took the dusty road at a run, not stopping to catch my breath until I got to the top of the hill.

Turning in a circle, I scanned the woods but couldn't see Smithers anywhere. It was as if he had melted into the trees and become part of the forest. But I could feel him and knew he was out there somewhere, standing stone-still, watching me and laughing.

Did I have time to go on? I checked the watch. It was only a few minutes past one. I still had almost an hour.

Not far down the other side of the hill, I lost track of the road as it dwindled into only a ragged path twisting through the woods.

I kept going, following the path until it led me out of the trees and into the glare of the hot afternoon sun. Rubbing my eyes against the biting light, I found myself standing at the edge of a high grassy meadow. I knew I should whistle for Smithers, but something about the lonesome quiet of the place stopped me.

It wasn't until my eyes adjusted to the brightness that I noticed the old homesteader's cabin tucked against the side of the hill not twenty yards across the field from me.

Cautiously, I stepped back into the cover of the forest. Darkness filled the two small windows at the front. The back of the building was shaded. No cars. No animals. Any paint that had once covered the little cabin had long since peeled away, and a thick patch of briers grew up one wall, climbing as high as the roof. Except for a few barn swallows that dipped in and out of the sagging eaves of the porch, nothing moved.

Still hidden in the trees, I whistled, softly at first and then as loudly as I could. "Smithers!" I called, twisting the watch back down to my wrist. It was getting late. Time was running out. I had to go back.

I whistled again, then waited.

All I could hear were bird songs swinging over the grass, and a faint whooshing sound, like wind through a long tunnel. Whoosh . . . whoosh. It came and went, came and went, almost like breathing.

I backed farther into the shadows.

The thick tree trunks on the other side of the clearing stood guard on the rest of the forest. Something was odd about the way the light fell on the woods. It made my eyes play tricks on me, and I thought I saw a figure—gray around the edges and dimmer than the rest of the dark forest—leaning against one of the trees.

Even the birds had quieted. But still, the whoosh . . . whoosh.

A gust of wind brushed over the meadow and swept up into the trees, stirring the heavy limbs of the old firs. They waved ghostly shadows along the ground. A cloud moved in front of the sun and spread darkness across the clearing as if a huge blanket was being pulled up over the grass. Goosebumps crawled over my shoulders and down my spine. Suddenly, I was very sure that whatever it was I was looking at was looking back at me.

I forgot about Smithers. I forgot about the cabin, and I stepped back, slowly at first and then at a thundering run—heading toward the gate on the other side of the hill.

By the time I reached the gate, I was gasping for air. I swung my leg over the top rail and looked up the empty road behind me.

I didn't know what to do about Smithers. How could I have been so stupid as to let him take off like that again? And where had he gone? My heart sank as I thought of what was going to happen if Sage found him before I did.

I felt around in my pocket for my arrowhead, relieved to discover that I hadn't lost it, too. But when I glanced down at my wrist to check the time, I realized I had lost something more than Smithers. Now Jack's watch was gone.

Chapter
16

I ran all the way back to the spot where I'd left Circe. When I got there—wouldn't you know it?—Squint was there, too. And so was Smithers. As soon as he saw me, he scampered over and jumped to paw at my stomach. He seemed so happy to see me, I couldn't get mad.

"How'd you find him?" I said, kneeling to let him lick my cheek.

Circe grinned. "I didn't find him," she said, nodding sideways at Squint, who was sitting close beside her busily poking holes in the dirt with a stick. "He did."

Squint looked up and smiled mischievously, his eyes dancing.

"We've been waiting for ages," Circe scolded. "What took you so long? You didn't get lost again, did you?"

"No, I wasn't lost," I said, suddenly remembering the watch. Casually, I put my hands behind my back, hoping she wouldn't notice. "You should have called me."

"Maybe she thought you were like Smithers and wouldn't come when she called." Squint laughed and drew a line in the dirt between two of the holes. "Besides, she wanted to see if you could find your way alone."

As soon as we got back to the house, we tied Smithers to the post on the porch. I looked around for Jack and was relieved when I didn't see him.

"I have to see how TomDog is," said Circe as she headed down the front steps. "Want to come along?"

Smithers must have thought she was talking to him because he perked his ears and pulled against the chain. "No, boy, no," I said, and stopped to scratch him on the head. "You stay put this time." Dejected, he lowered his tail and sat back down on his haunches.

"He'll be fine," said Circe. "Come on. It won't take long."

With the sun at our backs, the three of us crossed the yard, our stretched-out shadows climbing the front of the old gray barn. "Follow me, you guys," Circe said. "We'll take a short cut through here to the shearing shed."

The tall barn door swung open, slowly and wide. "Sage and Uncle Jack moved all the animals out of here the day of the earthquake," she explained as Squint took hold of my hand and led me inside. The door closed heavily behind us, its hinges creaking like old bones.

Inside, the barn was dark and stuffy, different from how most barns should be, I thought.

I had been inside only two others before. One belonged to a friend of Papa D's who raised almonds and dairy cows near Marysville. Its rafters rose two stories over my head, so high and open that swallows nested along the ridges. At first, the sour smell of the barn had burned inside my nose so strongly I thought it would stick there forever. But by the time we left, I didn't even notice it anymore. All I could smell was hay.

I visited another barn on a field trip with my fourth-grade class. That one was so clean you could see your reflection in the metal buckets they used to wash the concrete floor. That barn smelled like hay, too. But what I remembered most about both of those barns, more than the smell of hay, was the warm yellow light that filled them up.

I remembered leaning against one of the horse stalls while the teacher talked, thinking how much that light reminded me of a movie I had seen once, about Noah and how he built the ark for all the animals before the flood. There was a scene in that movie, a scene inside the ark after the rain had stopped. The first sun was filtering in through high windows onto the manger where the animals were lying and—even though it was only a movie—the light was warming the inside of the ark so much that I could almost feel it.

I was sure that was the way all the barns in the world must be, almost heavenly and filled with that same warm light.

But not the Matheson barn. Inside, it was low and narrow and dark, and mean.

The tin roof banged the heat right in on top of us, baking the inside of the place like a bread oven. But there wasn't any light. The spaces were cluttered and tight and dark.

Broken tools, empty boxes, and odd scraps of lumber filled the corners. I stepped over an old saddle that had been thrown on the floor. Everything seemed to be in a state of crumbling decay.

It was a lonely, dying, dirty place, and even though it was hot, it chilled me.

A draft ran over my feet, and a sudden gust of wind heaved against the side of the barn. The whole building whistled and rattled.

"Jack says it isn't safe in here anymore. He said the earthquake loosened the beams in this part of the building."

A narrow passage connected the barn to the shearing shed. It was lined with a string of little stalls on either side, like classrooms off a long school hallway—or the rooms off the hall at the hospital.

Even before we got to TomDog's pen, I heard him growl. It was a low throaty sound but weak and tormented, and full of worry. "Poor thing," said Circe. "He doesn't even know why he's growling."

Although I understood that it is usually fear that makes animals mean, the sound of TomDog's growl made me believe her. It had a senile tone about it, as if the dog knew he was supposed to make a noise but couldn't quite remember how.

Circe opened the low gate on the pen. "He won't hurt you," she assured me. "He hasn't the strength."

The old black dog was almost lost in the corner shadows of the small stall, lying like an uncomfortable knot on a bed of hay and blankets. Circe knelt down beside him and ran a gentle hand over his head until he was quiet.

Still holding my hand, Squint led me into the pen. "He's ashamed is all. That's what makes him mad. Sometimes he's so sore he can't get up, and he messes himself." The dog raised one white-tipped ear to us. His tail flopped weakly.

Squint pulled me closer. "He doesn't know you, but put your hand out for him to smell. You can pet him if you want."

Circe looked up at me as she continued caressing TomDog's bony head. "To tell you the truth, I don't think he recognizes me most of the time. But all I have to do is put out my hand, and he remembers."

"Pet him on the head. He likes that," said Squint.

"Scratch behind his ears. He can't work his back leg good enough to itch his fleas anymore." Squint moved close to the dog and smoothed the hair on his back. I pulled away. The last thing I wanted to do was touch that dying dog.

"Look. He ate some of the food I gave him."

"It doesn't look like he ate anything, Circe. He's going to die soon anyway, isn't he?"

"No." Circe glared at her brother. "He's not going to die for a long, long time if I have anything to say about it."

Squint stroked TomDog's matted coat. "Jack says he's going to die soon because he's old."

"He doesn't know what he's talking about. Jack just hates him for not getting his dying over with. It's easier for him to pretend TomDog's already dead. But just because he's old doesn't mean he should get tossed out like an empty soda bottle."

"I didn't say throw him out. All I said was he's going to die. He's too sick to get better." Squint stared down at his lap and quietly examined a piece of straw.

Hot sparks of anger lit Circe's eyes. "Why don't you just leave us alone and go hide in the woods! Since you're so sure he's going to die, you might as well just go fetch Jack's gun and blow a hole in his head yourself!"

Squint backed away from Circe and TomDog and squatted in the corner of the stall. The way I saw it, Squint was probably right. Poor old TomDog looked as if his remaining hours could be counted on one hand. But somehow he didn't look like he cared if he died. He just seemed happy to have someone keeping him company.

Squint scooted back beside his sister, nudging close to her. He set his head on her shoulder and kissed her cheek. "Don't be mad at me, Circe. I know. It's like with me. You're just taking care of him until his angel comes."

***

Except for a few buzzards circling lazily over the woods, the ranch was as still as the dust settling in the afternoon heat. "What time is it?" Circe asked as she latched the door on the barn.

Remembering the watch, I pretended I hadn't heard her, and I ran ahead toward the house to catch up with Squint.

Sage rode into the yard. He was dragging something on a rope behind his horse. "Coyote did this!" he yelled. "Get your uncle out here, Squint. He's in the house."

"What the heck is that?"

"It used to be a sheep," said Circe as she came up the steps after me.

"Not just 'a sheep,'" Jack boomed, slamming the screen as he thundered out onto the porch. "That's what is left of a damn fine ewe. Getting so you can't raise any animals but cattle, with all the predators we've got moving in on us. Government's protecting everything from bugs to birds these days. Can't trap, can't poison, can't shoot. What do they expect us to do, put our livestock on leashes and take them for walks every day? Hardly seems a point to this life anymore." He took the stairs in one stride and hurried over to Sage.

We watched from the porch as the two men pulled the dead sheep past the barn and down the hill on the other side of the shearing shed, the buzzards drifting with them.

Chapter
17

It was dinnertime, but it was still hot. Colleen had left the doors open, and flies raced in circles through the middle of the front hall. The smell of fresh paint bit into my nostrils as I followed Circe into the dining room.

"She's been redecorating again." Circe smirked, waving her hand in a wide arc. "Be careful what you touch. There's probably wet paint everywhere. I don't know why she bothers with this old place. The whole thing's going to fall down before she ever finishes." Circe went to the sideboard and took out a handful of silverware. "Jack keeps telling her not to waste her time, but she doesn't listen. Lord knows he gave up on the place ages ago. But Colleen says houses are like women—dress them up once in a while and the hard life won't show their age too soon. I figure she likes to mess with changing the house since she can't seem to change Squint or me."

She handed me the forks and spoons, and I walked

behind her, setting them around the table. It wasn't until then that I noticed the vase full of roses in the center. They looked like the same ones Jack had thrown on the compost pile that morning.

"Hey, Rudy!" Squint ran in from the kitchen. "They're talking about you on the radio! The man said your name."

Colleen was close behind him, wiping her hands on the tail of her shirt. "Well, at least we know your family is all right. Of course, they're looking for you. I don't quite understand it, though." She stopped by the window and looked outside. "They said the sheriff was heading up the search, but nowhere near here." Colleen turned to me with a questioning glance. "Didn't your parents know where you were going?"

"No," I answered sheepishly, trying not to meet her eyes. "I didn't exactly tell them I was leaving. . . ."

"Well." She sighed. "It's a good thing Jack didn't try to get to town this morning. The man on the radio said the bridge has been closed since the earthquake." She nodded at me sympathetically. "No one will be allowed to cross in either direction until tomorrow."

On her way back to the kitchen, Colleen paused to look out the window again, searching the sky past the top of the barn. She breathed a low whistle. "Good heavens, I hope Jack doesn't catch sight of that. . . ."

We all gathered around her to see what she was looking at. She pointed toward the sky where it met the ridge behind the barn. Even from that distance, I could make out the familiar sweeping wings of a golden eagle.

"Raccoons in the fruit trees, rabbits in the garden. Jack will shoot it for sure if he sees it, no matter if it's lambing season or not."

In a rush, we followed Colleen out onto the porch to watch the eagle take the breeze and glide, its wings spreading into wide-set feathered fingertips.

"I've only seen an eagle carry off a lamb once," Colleen said, her hands on her hips. "But Jack couldn't get a steady aim that time, so the bird got away." She tossed back her long black hair and almost laughed. "Poor Jack, nearly fell out of his side of the truck trying—leaned clear through the window waving that gun, aiming to get it into his sights. . . ." A sly grin formed on her face. "Don't usually make it my business, but I suppose—just that one time—I might have taken the turn in the road a wee bit fast."

Stunned, I asked, "You mean he tried to shoot an eagle?"

"No sheep rancher takes kindly to their stock being carried off by anyone." She spoke with a tone of resolve in her voice. "Even if the rustler is an eagle, and even if it is a federal crime."

The eagle spiraled higher and higher, then swooped down into the treetops where she blended with the dark green forest. As I lost sight of her, it suddenly occurred to me how long it had been since I'd thought of Papa D.

Colleen turned to go back inside. The screen door slammed behind her, but the rest of us stayed on the porch. Circe and Squint were quiet, both of them staring into the sky as if they were trying to wish the eagle back.

"To my mind," Circe said half under her breath, "ravens and crows are worse. They're scavengers. Take a newborn lamb's eyes and leave it to die. Like some people in this world, take what they want and turn their back on the rest. No crow never needed no lamb's eyes to stay alive."

***

Between worries about how I was going to get home and fear for the life of the eagle we'd seen, I had almost

95

forgotten about Jack's watch by the time we sat down to eat. It wasn't until Sage put his gun on the table that I remembered and quickly lowered my arm into my lap. I realized I would have to make sure where Sage was tomorrow before I went back to the meadow. I didn't want to be surprised to find him nesting in some tree along the road, spying on me like an old hoot owl waiting for his dinner.

He picked up the bowl of potatoes and was about to pass it across to me when the china cupboard started to rattle and the room began to shake. The rose vase tipped, then righted itself. Water slopped onto the table. Overhead, the timbers between the floors groaned stiffly.

"Aftershock!" Colleen's elbows, like springs, pushed her away from the table. She was on her feet in one motion, taking two steps to the sideboard and scooping up her grandmother's soup tureen.

Caught midmouthful, Circe lurched forward to steady the roses. I tried to duck under the table but was only partway there, my behind still stuck at table level, when the shaker stopped.

"Any damage?" Jack shouted through the silence that followed. The china cabinet offered a final shudder.

Noticeably flustered, Colleen returned to her chair.

Jack didn't seem worried by the little quake, only annoyed, striking a look of bother on his face as if he was waiting for a cramp in his stomach to pass. "Settle down, Colleen. They get smaller every time. It's natural to have a series of minor shocks after a big one like we had the other day."

"I'm just getting this place put together. I don't need my life shook up all the time like this."

Jack served himself a spoonful of potatoes. "These could go on for weeks. You might as well get used to them."

Colleen spread her napkin over her lap. "I'll never get used to them." She sighed. "Squint, would you like some salad to go with that meat you're not eating?" She raised the bowl to pass it to him, but Squint wasn't paying attention. If he was, he kept it to himself, making imaginary lines back and forth between the tip of his knife, his glass of milk and the salt shaker in front of his plate. More dot-to-dots. Over and over again.

Circe glanced at me, tossing me an I-told-you-he-was-backward look.

"Duncan MacLeod!" Colleen slapped her napkin down beside her plate, startling Squint into finally looking up. When he did, she said more calmly, "I'm asking if you want more salad. Are you finished? You hardly ate a thing, honey. Don't you like the roast? You've left half of it on your plate."

"Not hungry."

"You feeling bad? You're not coming down with a virus, are you?" She started to push back her chair and go to him.

"No, I'm okay. Maybe I can give the rest of my dinner to TomDog instead?"

Colleen was quiet, wiping a little spot of gravy from the table beside her plate with the tip of her napkin. I could tell she was avoiding Jack's eyes, working to think of some answer for Squint before Circe said anything about the dog.

"Fine. Save it for him, but finish your zucchini before you leave the table."

"That old dog doesn't have enough teeth left to eat mush," Jack said. "I don't know what makes you think he'll be able to take on that hunk of meat."

"TomDog is lots better tonight," Circe interrupted. "Uncle Jack, I just know he's going to be fine by tomorrow." I could tell she was eager to argue with him.

"We'll see . . . we'll see," Jack said absently, never

looking up from his plate. He just kept on filling his fork and chewing. Across the table, Circe fumed silently, staring at him with cold eyes.

I was uncomfortable sitting in the middle of what seemed like one family squabble after another, but as they went on, I was grateful there was something to keep Jack's mind off asking me about the watch.

I hoped the next day Squint would disappear after breakfast the way he had that morning. Then I'd have a reason to go snooping around in the woods again. But how was I going to get away from Circe long enough to go back to the place where I'd seen the cabin?

I tried to think what my grandfather would have done in my place, but I couldn't figure it. Papa D wouldn't have gone over the gate and lost the watch in the first place, any more than my own father would have.

"Rudy, would you mind passing the gravy down to this end?" Jack cleared his throat. "You off in a dreamland with Squint this evening?"

"Sorry," I said, my cheeks burning with embarrassment. "I didn't hear you at first."

Sage stared at me over his water glass. "Something on your mind, kid?"

Colleen reached across the table to touch my arm. "All this bickering has to be upsetting. I can't blame you for being distracted. You must be worried about when you're going home."

"Uh-huh." I swallowed. She didn't know my real worry was that someone might be living in that cabin I'd seen. "I was . . . I was wondering . . ."

"Yes?" asked Sage.

"I was wondering . . . does anyone else live on this side of the river?"

He put his fork on the plate. "Like who?"

"I don't know. Other ranchers? Summer people, maybe?"

Sage's face clouded over. "What makes you think there might be other folks out here?"

Looking away, I shook my head. "I didn't. I just wondered if anybody else was stuck over here like me."

Jack let out a relieved chuckle. "Oh, I see. Afraid not, Rudy. No one else lives this far out. The county road stops at our front gate. We're the end of the line, unless you count that old cabin on the south road. But nobody goes there anymore. It isn't safe. Too tempting a place to play."

With that, we all returned to eating our dinner quietly, all of us, that is, except Squint, who was once again making invisible patterns with his silverware.

Chapter
18

That night Squint was sleeping before I even crawled under the covers. I lay wide-eyed for a long time, tossing and worrying, trying to wrestle out a plan for getting back to the meadow to find Jack's watch.

Somehow, I'd have to get away by myself. And it would have to be early, before anyone else was awake.

An elbow of moonlight slanted across the wall above Squint's bed. It reminded me of the wall in my room at home—the same wall where Mom and Dad had wanted to put Papa D's bed when he got out of the hospital.

"It will be fine," Dad had said. "Papa D won't bother you at all."

Papa D, living with us—it was a wish I'd had for as long as I could remember.

In the week before they let me visit him, I spent hours alone, imagining how my room would look with Papa D's things in it. I pictured his bed, the low cot he slept on after my grandmother died, with the red Mexican serape neatly smoothed over the edges. Above it we would hang the case that held his arrowhead collection. I couldn't wait for my room to take on the sweet scent of his pipe tobacco, the way everything in his old house had.

But when I saw him in the hospital, I realized it wouldn't be that way at all. My room wouldn't be cluttered and noisy like the dusty corners of Papa D's old house. His belongings wouldn't be there any more than he would.

Before I got to the parking lot that day, even before the smell of the hospital had left me, I decided to tell my parents that I'd changed my mind. I didn't want to share my room with Papa D after all.

***

I came awake with a start, tangled in my sheets. I sat up and looked around the room, knowing I'd overslept again. The sun was too high for it to be early morning. Squint's bed was already empty, and I could hear the muffled sounds of conversation drifting up from the kitchen.

I'd had a dream . . . not a nightmare exactly but a bad dream that left me uneasy and shaken.

Had I dreamed about going home? Or Smithers? Or the watch?

The watch . . . if I went downstairs while they were eating, I knew I'd probably get stuck with Circe all day and never get a chance to look for it alone, so I decided to wait—let everyone think I was still sleeping—until they'd all gotten busy with their usual routines.

I rolled over to look out the window. Without warning, the memory of the dream rushed into me like a cold wind, leaving a heavy ache in my chest.

In the dream Papa D and I had been hiking uphill to a

102

grassy knoll, like the one above our camp at the river. The grass was green and tall and smelled like spring. Far below us on the hillside, newborn lambs were clumped with their mothers, grazing in little dots. I remember feeling the chill of the evening fog on my face as we began to search the darkening sky for eagles.

I heard her cry long before I saw her. It was a melancholy sound, lonesome and forlorn, as if she were the only creature left in the world.

From high in the treetops she swooped, her wings cutting deep strokes in the wind above the fog. The eagle floated for a moment, then tucked her wings against her body and sped like a bullet toward the earth.

As I watched her fall, I remembered I tried to scream. I was trying to scream a warning—not a warning to the lambs that grazed unaware beside their mothers. No, I was trying to scream at the eagle.

But in a dream, a scream is nothing; there isn't any sound, only a desperate, terrifying silence.

As the eagle rose into the evening sky, a silhouette of feathers with the lamb clutched beneath her, a blast of rifle fire rang out from somewhere in the distance.

I turned to my grandfather to hide my eyes at his chest. But as I did, he backed away and stood behind me, stiff and silent and gray as a stone.

I heard the slow whine of the kitchen door downstairs. Footsteps crossed the porch. The kitchen was emptying.

I left the bedroom quickly, hoping I could make it out the front door without Colleen noticing me. It was so late she would probably be painting in the dining room by now anyway.

Chapter
19

Circe passed me on the stairs, long awake and already dirty, her face more drawn down at the edges than it had been the night before. I paused on the step to let her pass. Something was wrong, and even before she spoke, I had a feeling I knew what it was.

She stopped a couple of steps above me and then turned, looking down at me over her shoulder. A stray flake of hay fell from her hair, drifting to her shoulder where it settled below the collar of her blouse. She brushed it away with an impatient swipe of her hand.

"He put TomDog down," she spit coldly, hesitating for a moment as if expecting me to respond. But all I could do was stand nervously shuffling on the stair, not knowing what to say, wishing I'd waited a while longer to get out of bed.

"You might look for Squint," she said, then continued up the steps. "If you find him, see if he's okay. I told him I didn't want to play the game today."

From where I stood she looked like someone twice her

age. She turned to walk to the landing at the top of the stairs, taking each step as if she was carrying a heavy load across her back, her right arm limp at her side, her left grasping the stair rail for support.

More than ever I wished I was good at finding the right words to say, but I turned away and hurried down the stairs so I wouldn't hear her cry.

Downstairs, the house was hushed, and for the first time since I'd been there, I heard my own footsteps as I crossed the floor in the front hall.

A hazy shaft of sunlight fell drearily through the window in the kitchen, where Colleen was sweeping crumbs from the table into her hand.

Would she ask me about Circe? Would she expect me to say something about TomDog—something grown-up about what had happened?

I stood quietly in the doorway watching her. As she worked, she missed a few crumbs, and they drifted like snowflakes to the floor. Maybe she was feeling it, too—the need for silence, the not-knowing-what-to-say feeling I had. She was bowed, concentrating hard on her task, moving her arms methodically across the leaves of the table, back and forth in long, exhausted strokes. Although I guessed she knew I was there, she didn't look up until I was well into the room.

"Morning, Rudy. There's a plate of bacon on the drainboard. Help yourself to cereal. Sorry we haven't been able to contact your folks yet."

I nodded, and walked quickly past her to the counter, grabbed a few pieces of bacon, and headed for the back door.

The washing machine churned loudly in the mud room as I walked through. I knew Smithers would be around front, tied to the porch.

It was hot out, and sticky, the way it gets in summer before a storm. Even the chickens were hiding in the shaded places under the porch and against the buildings, where they pecked restlessly at the dirt. The flies were out, too, thick and buzzing my face like dive bombers. Papa D always used to say you could tell rain was on its way by the number of flies you could kill with one swat. The tick-tick-tick of Jack's sprinklers lulled the morning air, a white spray of water arching lazily back and forth over his garden.

I guess I had known Jack would do it, put TomDog down, that is, even though Circe insisted he was getting better. Thinking back, Jack's not getting mad at her about TomDog the night before was almost as if he was saying he'd already made up his mind what he was going to do. It practically made sense to me that if something was dying it was your job to do the merciful thing and put it out of its misery.

Funny, though. Remembering how TomDog looked when I saw him, he hadn't seemed all that miserable to me. Humiliated maybe, but not miserable.

I walked around the house to the front porch, thinking I'd find Smithers there. The water bowl was freshly filled, but he wasn't tied to the post as usual.

The screen door banged behind me, and I jumped. Colleen came out onto the porch with a broom. Positioning herself in front of me, she started working her way in my direction, whooshing dirt clouds onto the stairs with so much energy it seemed she was trying to sweep me off with them.

"Guess you saw Circe head upstairs," she said. "Likely she'll keep to herself most of the day. Circe's an angry child and doesn't do well with grief. Can't really blame her, betrayed so many times like she's been. . . ." For a moment her voiced trailed off into the muggy morning air. "If you're looking for something to do, you're welcome to go out and watch the men. They're over in the barn, building a box for that poor old dog."

Although something morbid in me wanted to see what had happened to TomDog, I had another mission more important than watching Jack and Sage pound a coffin together, and if I didn't hurry I was going to lose my chance.

"Have you seen Smithers?" I asked.

She went on sweeping as she spoke. "I don't know where he is now, but I saw him out here earlier. Squint fed him a pancake after breakfast. Better ask Jack or Sage where he is. Won't do to have him running loose."

I stepped off the porch into the sun and whistled for him. Over the yard, ripples of high-feathered clouds hung hot and white. They held the air still. To the south, cumuli were building on the horizon. I whistled again, then waited, ready to set into a real panic if he didn't come.

Then, like a guilty little kid, Smithers crawled out from beneath the chicken coop and galloped over to me. Could it be that he was at last learning to come when I called him?

The big double doors of the barn were open. From across the yard, I could hear Jack's curses rising between hammer falls. If I didn't want them to see me, I was going to have to cut behind the building, up the side of the hill in back of the barn below the big pepperwood tree.

Smithers and I crossed the yard and sneaked around the barn, passing the tree and the back corral before we got to the shearing shed.

I'd forgotten about the other dogs. They let off an alarm so loud you'd have thought a marauding bear was rumbling through. "Come on, Smithers!" I said, grabbing him by the collar and hurrying to the corner of the shed. The open field between us and the woods was empty, and we made a run toward the road. We were almost free and clear when someone yelled at me.

"Hey! Hold up there, kid!"

It was Sage. He'd seen us, but we didn't stop. Instead, I headed up the road at a run, hoping he would think I hadn't heard him.

I didn't stop running until Smithers and I were in the cover of the trees. The sky above the tall firs was filled with white glare. Sweat had gathered in the hollow place at my throat and was beginning to creep down my chest. I waited there, hidden in the shadows, holding Smithers and catching my breath, until I was sure no one was coming after us.

Chapter
20

As I climbed over the wobbly gate, it surprised me how breaking rules a second time seemed so much easier than the first. I suppose the worry wasn't so deep since I knew I'd already gotten away with it once. Besides, Smithers had already slipped under the bottom rail and, for a change, was waiting for me to join him on the other side.

I'm not sure how long it took me to get up the hill, stooped over like an old man, staring at the dirt without finding Jack's watch. It seemed like ages, especially out in the open the way I was. For all I knew, Sage could be right behind me. And Smithers, although he was sticking by me, was getting nervous and jumpy, lifting his ears every moment or so to look toward the woods and whimper. He seemed more anxious than I was to get off the road.

But when we started down the path toward the meadow, something made me stop and reach into my pocket for my arrowhead. "Please let me find it," I whispered, clutching the stone as if I was afraid I'd lose it, too.

By the time we finally got to the meadow, I'd almost given up. It felt like it was way past lunchtime, but the sun hadn't reached that side of the hill yet, and dew still clung to the grass. The little cabin was draped in morning shadows and seemed even more gloomy and lonesome than it did yesterday.

I half expected to see the same shadow in the woods I'd seen before, but nothing seemed to be spying on me from the trees. There were no signs of life at all. Even the birds must have known a storm was coming and had already taken to the close-in branches of the trees. Everything in the forest was tucked in, waiting for rain.

I whistled softly for Smithers, to keep him close, then stepped out into the meadow. The grass was still matted in the place where I'd been standing the day before. I knelt down and ran my hand over it.

Where could the watch be? I had examined the ground so carefully. How could I have missed it?

A cloud's shadow crawled across the grass, up the hillside, and into the trees. The deep edge of the forest seemed to shrink around the meadow as the light changed. Overhead, the sky turned the color of elephant hide, and across it the clouds folded into themselves like thick, heavy skin. Suddenly the air was alive with electricity. Rain was on the wind. I could taste it.

Smithers stopped just ahead of me and stood rigid, listening. I heard it then, too—the same windy thump I had heard the day before. Whoosh . . . whoosh, that faint rushing sound, like fast water falling over a rocky ledge.

A breeze swept the sound uphill away from us, and it was quiet again. But Smithers shook nervously beside me. I drew him close to me, feeling his quivering, excited body, ready to run. "What is it, boy?" I asked.

The wind turned and brought the whooshing sound

back to us, but with it came a new sound, outside the first one. It was a high, whistling, melancholy call, almost a song. Yes, I thought, as if someone was humming a tune from high in the trees.

Smithers's ears stood up. His paws worked the dirt anxiously, skittering around my legs.

Across the meadow the grass quivered under only a breath of a breeze, and the song came again. That high sing-song humming. Ghostlike, unnatural, it sailed over the field toward us until it seemed to be all around, echoing off the trees. Beside me, Smithers sputtered on his toes, unable to keep still.

Then, before I could tell where it was coming from, the song was cut off by the wind. It swung away from us and was gone. Something wasn't right about the place. Quickly, I scanned the ground in one last attempt to find the watch.

It wasn't cold, but all at once I was chilled through to my insides. There, sitting in the dirt beside my left foot, rolled in a tight shiny ball, was one of the unmistakable wads of foil left over from a piece of Sage's violet candy.

I swung around, sure he'd be standing behind me with his gun. "Forget the watch," I said out loud. "I'll tell Jack I lost it. I just won't say where." I tugged on Smithers's collar, dragging him back to the cover of the trees.

We took off on the path running. Without warning, the woods filled up with a flash of light, turning the trees around us into flat, black silhouettes.

Thunder roared across the valley like a freight train. It came on top of us, and somewhere close by, a tree splintered in a flash and a bang.

Smithers yelped and leaped in a startled sideways hop, crashing through the brush. Without turning to see the tree, I ran with him, hard, as great wedges of light cut through the forest, leaving me running blind.

Chapter
21

It was raining and cold by the time we got back to the house, and although it was only just past noon, the lights were on. A white tail of smoke fought the wind above the chimney.

With her hands in her jean pockets, Circe met me at the door. "Where were you?" she glared at me. "We looked all over for you. Your parents—"

Colleen opened the door wide. "Look what we have here!" she laughed. "Where in blue blazes have you been? Do you have Squint with you? Your parents called twice while you were out."

"The phone's working?"

"They're in town. Jack's got the number. He's trying them now." She handed me a towel.

The wind whipped the house with a vengeance. Jack came up behind Colleen. "Get this damn door closed, will you! Wind's blowing rain all over the floor." He looked down at me, shaking his head. "You look terrible, boy. I'll put Smithers in the shed with the others till the storm passes. You'd better get in here and dry off. I tried to reach your folks, but the phone's gone down again." The lights inside the house flickered as I toed-off my mud-wrapped shoes.

Inside, the house was full of the warm smells of Colleen's cooking. Sage was tucked up close to the hearth, warming his feet by the fire and puffing a cigarette. Even from my side of the room, I could see fresh, raw scratches on his arm.

I avoided him, wondering how he could have been at the meadow watching me. He didn't look as if he'd been out in the storm. In fact, he looked as if he'd been planted in that chair for hours.

He looked around sharply at me as I walked into the room. "Where have *you* been? You strayed off the road or something? You're as bad as your dog, the way you disappear. Brought him with you, didn't you?" He paused to flick the ash from his cigarette. "You should know better than to take off in a storm. No one's going to hunt you down in weather like this." Sage took a long draw on his smoke and blew it out slowly. It floated across the room, then hovered over the roses that were wilting in the middle of the dining table.

When Jack returned from the dog pen, he settled in by the fire across from Sage. The fear I felt in the meadow seemed far away. The house was snug and cheerful, blanketing all of us from the storm outside. Colleen made hot chocolate for me, and Circe and I sat at the table working on a jigsaw puzzle. She didn't mention TomDog.

The lights flickered again, and Colleen began to set candles in strategic spots around the room. "If it wasn't for the peace and privacy of wide open spaces," she said, sighing, "I'd trade in this pioneer life for a nice tract home in the suburbs with a swimming pool and cable TV."

Jack winked at her from across the room. "Sure, hon. And you could work nine to five like your mama, and I could sit in commuter traffic every night. . . ." He shifted his gaze to me. "By the way, Rudy, I'd like to make sure to get my watch back before you go home."

I didn't hear the storm outside anymore. Suddenly it was inside my head. The watch. I'd forgotten all about it. What was I going to say now? Jack set his book aside and pulled himself up out of the chair.

"I don't have it with me," I said, not knowing whether to stay or run. I swallowed back the urge to lie and tell him it was upstairs or that I had left it out in the shed. I knew it wasn't going to do any good. I'd have to tell him I lost it; I just hoped the right words would come out.

"Did you leave it in Squint's room?" There was nothing but trust in his voice.

"I don't know where it is, sir. I haven't been able to find it since yesterday. . . . I think I lost it."

Jack didn't say anything at first. He looked hard at me, though, as if he would get mad if I was his own kid. He shook his head as he sank back down in his chair.

From his side of the room, Sage looked up and stared at me. He stared like he thought I was all wrong somehow, or maybe something about the whole world was wrong.

He leaned forward toward Jack, as if to share a secret, but reached into his back pocket and handed something to him.

"This what you're looking for?" he said, still glaring at me. "I found it this morning. Forgot to give it to you."

"Well, that's a relief. Where was it?"

There was a long pause. Then Sage turned to Jack, almost smiling. "In the shearing shed. Rudy must have let it slip off when he was helping Circe with the dogs."

I could hardly breathe. Why was Sage lying for me? He had to have found it somewhere past the gate. Was he the one I'd seen lurking in the trees yesterday, watching me? But how could it have been Sage? Hadn't he been with Jack when Circe and I went into the woods to look for Squint?

Jack let out a long sigh. "I suppose it was too big for you, wasn't it, Rudy?"

The words stuck like last night's dinner in my throat. "Yes, sir. I guess it was. I'm real sorry—"

"Never mind. Accidents happen. I'm just glad to have it back."

Sage kept smiling until Jack took up his book and started reading again. As soon as he did, the smile dropped from Sage's face and he leered across the room at me as if his smile had never been. The way darkness follows a flash of lightning, I forgot his smile so fast that I couldn't imagine it back.

Colleen stopped by Sage's chair to empty the ashtray. "I'll be out of your way as soon as the storm breaks," he said.

"No, Sage, you stay put. No need for you to go anywhere. The way it looks, Jack might need you to help hunt up Squint. I can't imagine what's keeping him out so long, and in this storm."

She circled the room, stopping to nervously adjust magazines on the coffee table. "I hate thunderstorms almost as much as earthquakes," she muttered as she stooped to straighten a stack of Squint's dot-to-dot projects. "Do you think we ought to try to find him now? He's been out there an awfully long time."

Circe shook her head. "There's no point. He's playing the game. He won't let you find him. He's mad because I wouldn't play today."

"Circe's right," said Jack. "Don't worry. A little weather never hurt anyone. He's probably holed up in one of his secret hiding places."

The rain let up after a while, but every few moments

118

the lights blinked with the wind. Colleen passed through the room, stopping at the counter to lift the receiver on the phone. She looked at me, shrugging her shoulders apologetically, as if to say she was sorry that the storm had come up and their phone was so unreliable.

But each time she did, I was filled with an unexpected pang of relief—I didn't want my parents to come too soon. I was sure when they did, Dad would be angry. But worse than that, I also knew we would have to stop to see Papa D on the way home.

Circe looked up from the puzzle. "I don't know where Jack thinks Squint's hiding places are," she muttered. "I've spent hours looking for him and haven't found one yet." She paused to gaze out the window into the storm.

"There hasn't been a thunder bumper like this in years, has there, Coll?" Jack mused. "This wind might just decide to take the roof off."

Colleen wasn't listening. She stopped at the window and rubbed a little circle on the steamy glass. "Don't you think we ought to do something, Jack? Maybe he's lost. Or hurt."

"Give him a while longer. He'll be fine."

"He might be scared."

"I don't like to say it, but maybe it'll cure him of skipping out the way he does. He might finally under-stand that no one likes to play this game of his."

"Rudy." Colleen turned to me, anxiety filling her eyes. "Are you sure you didn't see him anywhere?"

"No," I said. "I didn't see anyone. . . ." Sage squashed his cigarette in the ashtray and glared at me.

Colleen tried again. "He was good and upset about TomDog, you know. Maybe he's in the shearing shed with the dogs?"

Circe fidgeted with a puzzle piece. "He's not there. I already checked when I was looking for Rudy."

"Couldn't he be in the barn?" I said, offering the only suggestion I could think of.

Circe laughed. "No way. Squint knows it's off limits. He'd never go in there without permission."

"That's one thing you can count on with him." Jack nodded. "He never breaks the rules."

The worried expression stayed on Colleen's face as she stood by the window, biting her lower lip. "He's a smart boy. I can't understand why he'd stay out in the storm."

Jack put his book down and walked over to stand behind her. "Don't worry, Colleen. I'll take the dogs out after him if he's not back soon. You know Squint. The boy's a—"

Across the table from me, Circe twitched like a cat. "He's just a pain!" she suddenly fumed, and slammed her hands on the table. The puzzle flopped apart, stray pieces dancing off onto the floor. She shoved her chair backward and stood up. "He makes me crazy running off the way he does. . . . How could he expect me to play games all day after what happened this morning?" Her hand trembled at her mouth as she leveled her eyes at her aunt. "You should have sent him with my mother!" she screamed. "You should have sent him. . . ." Her words choked back in her throat, and she turned, running across the room and up the stairs.

The room lit up, and a clap of thunder crashed above the house just as Circe's bedroom door slammed. I watched the vase on the table wobble. Rose petals shook loose from the wilting blooms, gathering like ashes in the center of the table.

"You'll have to forgive her, Rudy." Colleen shook her head. "She doesn't mean it."

Jack sat back down in his chair. "It's your rotten sister's fault. She wasn't any better a mother to those two kids than that dog Jezebel is to her litter of pups."

"Jack, please," said Colleen.

"Well, it's no secret, is it? Woman like that high-tailing it and leaving them the way she did. Seems like everyone in your family takes flight. Circe . . . well, that girl ought to quit thinking she can solve the troubles of the world. She lets Squint pull her strings too much. She isn't his mother, you know."

I wanted to disappear like the steam off my hot chocolate. I was sure Colleen was going to cry right in front of me. I stared down at the puzzle. In that house I was no longer a stranger. I felt as tightly knotted up inside their lives as they were in each other's.

Colleen looked across the room toward Jack, who'd gone back to shuffling the pages of his book, then leaned across the table and took my hand, her eyes full of concern.

"Never mind any of what we're saying. Circe's had a bad day is all, what with TomDog's dying. This storm's got us all jumpy. It muddles the mind. She'll be down before long, her regular self. Then we'll all go out together to look for the boy."

By the time I heard Circe's door open upstairs, Jack was snoring in the chair, and I had long since given up on the puzzle and taken up one of Squint's drawing pads.

"I can't stand it up there," Circe said, loping down the stairs. "The wind's pounding so hard I can't think. It feels like the whole house is going to blow over. I'm going outside to call for him. Come with me, Rudy. He'll hear your whistle. It's louder than mine."

But out on the porch the wind made more noise than both of us put together. It was relentless, blowing an eerie whistle of its own.

"I can't make any sound," I said, spitting the rain out of my mouth.

Circe cupped her hands around her mouth. "DUN-

CAN!" she screamed.

Her face was a maze of worry and fear. "It's my fault. It's always my fault. I should have played the game with him today." She leaned against the porch rail and sighed. "It's my fault Mother left, you know."

A sudden windy blast whipped around the upper story of the house so hard that it vibrated the floor boards on the porch. Circe waited for it to die down. Then she went on talking, as if I wasn't there, as if she was letting her words out just so she could hear herself say them.

"Whenever Mama went out, she left me in charge. She'd say, 'Circe, be an angel. Keep an eye on the baby while I'm gone.' I hated it when she did that because it was against the rules for me to take him out of his crib, and he always cried.

"One day he started crying like mad and begging me. He kept saying, 'Circe, be angel.' He was used to me holding him when he cried. What was I supposed to do?"

A tear started working its way down Circe's cheek. She pretended it was rain and brushed it away.

"When my mother came home, we weren't doing anything wrong, just fooling with some blocks and cars. You know, little kid stuff. I didn't think she was mad. She didn't say a word about it, just made me put him back in the crib. Then she fed us dinner.

"But you know what she did the next day? Before I left for school, she said, 'See what I have to do now, angel?' She led me to Squint's crib and made me watch her tie him down to the mattress. When she was done, she sent me off to school."

Circe looked away from me and picked at one of her fingernails. Part of me wanted her to stop talking so I wouldn't have to watch her cry again. But more of me hoped she would go on.

"When I got home, she was gone. I could hear him wailing from out in the street. It was a terrible sound, the kind of sound a cat makes when it's stuck in a tree.

"I tried to untie him, but she'd made the knots too tight. I couldn't find any scissors, and he was thrashing so bad I was afraid to use a knife. I didn't know what else to do, so I climbed into the crib beside him and sang to him all night so he'd keep quiet. Sometime the next day I figured Mama wasn't coming back, so I called Auntie Coll, and she came and got us."

The wind had died, and a damp calm hung over the yard. It held her words in midair, like smoke. I couldn't think of what to say to comfort her, but for a change I didn't feel like I needed to say anything. We just stood there together, letting silence take up the space between us.

The lightning had moved toward the east, and only an occasional flicker dashed on the horizon now and then. Thunder chased it in a low rumble like marbles over a hollow board. The storm was moving away from us. Squint would be back soon, and perhaps the phone would work again.

Suddenly the calm was broken. Something cracked, then rumbled; and both of us looked across the yard.

Behind the barn, the gnarly old pepperwood tree buckled with another crack and slid down the hill, landing in a heap. Its huge limbs sliced into the roof of the barn like a knife into a loaf of bread. Timbers creaked, the air shuddered like a living thing, and the whole front half of the building slumped and folded into a shattered mound.

Chapter
22

"What in the devil's name was that?" Jack yelled, careening onto the porch. Sage and Colleen followed close behind him.

"It's the barn!" Circe screamed, pointing to the remains of the old building. "The tree fell!"

Before anyone could stop her, she was running across the muddy yard. Jack reached for his slicker. "Get back here, girl! It isn't safe! Hang on! Wait, will you? Stay clear of there, you hear me?"

Sage moved even faster than Jack, galloping through the mud after Circe. He was still in his slippers, which slopped mud onto the back of his pants as he ran.

He stopped Circe before she reached the corrals. I heard shouting, but their words were lost on the wind.

Colleen stood her ground, staring at the barn, her eyes stuck on the old broken tree. "Oh, my God" was all she said, muttering it over and over to herself as if she'd forgotten that I was standing beside her.

All at once Colleen yanked my shirt and pulled me

close to her. She let out a small high noise, like a baby's whimper. For a moment I thought it was Smithers. Then I remembered Jack had put him in the shed with the other dogs.

She spun me around, and a look of horror swept her face. Standing there, she looked weak and clouded, as if she was about to be sick. Her hands shook, but she held me with her eyes, her voice covered with fear. "You don't really think Squint could be in there, do you?"

Before I could speak, Circe stumbled back to the house, her face streaming with tears. "Oh, Auntie Coll. Please tell me he couldn't be in there. He couldn't. He knows better. . . ." Colleen took Circe into her arms.

"Now, now, child. Everything's going to be all right." Colleen's voice sounded as unconvincing as my dad's when he talked about Papa D.

"I didn't hear him. Squint would call out if he was in there, wouldn't he? If he could . . ."

The barn was a shambles. The tree lay across it, its limbs sticking up like the bones of a bombed-out building. Sage was leaving the shed with a chain saw. He shouted something to Jack. Jack waved. He had the horses haltered and following behind him.

Colleen's weathered hand smoothed Circe's hair. She was calm again, like the calm that came with the end of the storm. "Honey, Squint's going to be fine. You know, you were probably right. There's only a slim chance he's in there. But if he is, Jack and Sage will get him out. Look," she said, pointing to the wreckage, "they're going to cut away the tree." She paused and took a deep breath. "Let's go inside until—"

Circe pulled away from her aunt. "No," she said. "I want to watch."

She stood beside me as the roar of the chain saw ripped into the muggy air, sending oily smoke up behind Sage in black puffs.

"Go ahead if you want," Colleen said. "But it's too much worry for me." She opened the screen door, then waved me over. "Sage doesn't even have his jacket, Rudy. Would you mind taking it to him?"

As I watched the men work, fear grew in my stomach. What would they find beneath the broken timbers and shattered limbs? If Squint was hurt, or worse (could I even imagine?) dead . . . I didn't want to be standing there. I wanted to be back in the house beside the fire working that puzzle, back in a time before all this had happened.

But I knew wishes weren't any better at making miracles than my arrowhead was, cold and lifeless in the bottom of my pocket.

I stood waiting for the sawing to stop before I offered Sage his jacket. He nodded a thank-you, then handed the chain saw over to Jack.

"Where'd you put that dog of yours? He's not messed up in this, too, is he?"

"No, sir," I said, shuddering even though the clouds were beginning to clear. "Jack put him in the shed. Should I do anything to help?"

"Yes. Give me a hand with this blasted thing."

I stepped into the branches of the fallen limb and crawled to the other side. Grunting under its weight, we carried the limb a few yards and dropped it with the other rubble.

"Thanks for telling Jack you found the watch in the shed," I said casually, hoping he wouldn't hear me.

Sage kicked the limb, and it rolled over on its side. "Don't thank me, kid. Squint's the one who told me to make sure you got it. He gave it to me this morning, before you were up. I tried to give it to you earlier, but you ran off up the hill."

I felt like I'd been shot. Dazed, I stood frozen, unable to move.

"Rudy!" Jack hollered at me. "Stand clear of there, back by the fence. You shouldn't be over here at all."

Colleen crossed the yard in short, nervous steps. She had a plastic garbage bag over her head even though it wasn't raining anymore. "Is he in there, Jack?" she asked urgently. "Is there any sign of him at all?"

"No," Jack said, looking back to survey the remains of the barn. "It will take a long time to clear away enough to really know. But I can't imagine he's there. That boy never broke a rule in his life."

A bad feeling slammed into me then, like a jolt of nausea or a knock on the head. Was I the only one who knew that Squint did break rules, at least the rule about not going past the gate?

"Rudy, get Circe, and the two of you check the shearing shed again. Look around. If we're lucky, maybe Squint's in there after all."

The shed was dark. The narrow slats on the sides let in a cold draft but no light. I peered anxiously into each one of the dark, steamy stalls that lined the passage, but there was no sign of Squint. I stopped to check Smithers, then went on.

Circe was quiet as she crept along in front of me, bending down every moment or so to get a closer look into the pens. She was checking them all carefully, but there was a new sense of resignation in her walk, more than I'd seen when she told me TomDog had died.

"Squint's back in that barn, I just know it," she said at last. "He has to be."

"No. He's all right, Circe," I blurted out. "I know he's safe."

"What makes you so sure?" She stopped a few feet ahead of me and turned, her voice suddenly calm.

"Because I think I know where he is."

Chapter
23

"I know you're wrong, Rudy. We shouldn't be out here. I ought to stay at the house. What if they find him?"

"Come on. Let's hurry."

"How do you know he's there?"

I reached into my pocket for my arrowhead. "I just know is all. Hurry up. I'll show you."

We headed up the muddy road at a run and were over the gate without another word. By then, I knew the path by heart and led Circe through the woods to the meadow.

It was the singing that stopped us.

Circe ran to the edge of the grass. "That's Squint! Rudy, that's him! Where is he? I can't see."

The sun was just coming back onto the hillside, shedding a hazy light over the little cabin. A thin, ghostly fog rose above the warming grass.

"He's got to be down there," I said, although I couldn't see him. "Listen."

The singing floated toward us up the little rise for another moment. Then it stopped. "He's there! Look!" Circe didn't wait for me. She ran down the hill. I followed her, slipping all the way on the wet grass.

Squint walked out of the shadows at the back of the cabin.

"How could you? How could you?" Circe screamed as she ran to him. By the time I caught up with them, her cheeks were an angry red.

Squint was soaked from head to toe, shivering in the shade of the little building. "I'm sorry, Circe," he said in a low voice. "Don't be mad. But when TomDog . . . I couldn't. . . ."

"TomDog?" she cried, tears streaking through the mud on her cheeks. "What's he got to do . . . ? Next time you pull a stunt like this I'll murder you, you little brat! Do you think I like running after you every day? Do you think I enjoy your stupid little game? I hate it!" She turned in the path and ran back up to the top of the hill. "I hate it! And I don't care if you run off and never come back. I'm sick of being your nursemaid!"

Squint stood in the path hugging himself, his arms wrapped tightly across his chest. Beneath his freckles, his face had gone an ashen gray. I could tell he wanted to cry but was probably too embarrassed, with me standing beside him. We watched Circe disappear into the woods.

"Are you all right, Squint?"

He didn't answer at first, nervously wiping his muddy shoes in the grass.

"She was just worried about you, is all. The barn fell in. Everyone was afraid you were inside."

"I didn't mean to stay. But I . . ." Squint leaned down to pick at his shoe. "I didn't want to see her, crying like she was about TomDog. I was trying to think what to say. . . ." He looked up at me, tears filling his eyes. "That

130

ever happen to you, Rudy? You ever want to make someone feel better so bad you can't even look at them?"

I stared down at him, suddenly realizing I still had my arrowhead in my hand. "Yes," I said, nearly choking on my words, "it's happened to me."

"I didn't mean to stay. I come out here sometimes, but I only come to see the bird."

"The bird?"

"Uh-huh. There's a cage . . . with an eagle. I'll show you if you want to see." Squint took hold of my hand and led me around the back of the cabin. His hand was small and cold, and he walked so close to me our sides were touching.

"You won't tell, will you, Rudy? I never went inside. Sage has a lock on it."

"Sage?"

"Uh-huh. He's the one who keeps her. I wanted to touch her feathers, look in her eyes. But I couldn't. He's got a hood tied over her head."

A tall wire fence had been built against the back of the house. The eagle was perched on a stump in the center of the enclosure, tethered to a limb by one foot. It was bright yellow. The other one was obviously injured. I walked softly beside Squint, but the eagle sensed we were there and shuffled clumsily on the stump. I had never been up close to a golden eagle before. She was a lot bigger than I expected, as tall as the top half of my body, and the most magnificent thing I'd ever seen. No wonder Sage hadn't wanted Smithers and me snooping around the woods!

As we approached the cage, the huge bird's wings whooshed out in an ungainly flutter.

"When the storm started, she got excited. She was thumping her wings. When she does that, sometimes I sing to calm her down. Circe used to do that for me when I was little." The eagle's covered head darted right and

131

left. "Do you know why she wears a hood?"

I had heard about hooding falcons to quiet them, so I told him I supposed it kept her from being afraid. "If she could see, she'd be frightened. She'd probably get frantic and want to fly. I guess it keeps her from hurting herself. What happened to her, anyway?"

Squint was suddenly quiet, making designs in the mud with the toe of his shoe. "Sage shot her down last spring during lambing season."

It wasn't hard at all for me to picture Sage moving through the trees like a wolverine, his shoulders bent forward, slinking along the forest floor in his heavy black boots and carrying that gun.

"I saw him do it. She came down near where I was playing. When he found her, she was sitting kind of sideways on the road. At first it looked like he was going to kill her. He knelt down beside her and pulled out his gun—like he was going to put her out of her misery. Like TomDog, you know. But he didn't. He put his head in his hands and just stared at her. Then he started swearing to himself and chucked the gun into the bushes by the road. After that, he took off his jacket and wrapped her up. He's had her here ever since."

The sun glinted off the bronze feathers on her shoulder, and I thought about the way Sage stared at me in the house earlier—how I'd imagined his look of disapproval was a look of meanness. I hadn't seen the true Sage at all, even after he'd lied about finding the watch.

I suddenly wondered if all truths about people were like that, hidden and kept secret from the rest of the world. Or maybe it was just that people were a lot like Squint's dot-to-dots. The parts might be there from the beginning, but sometimes the picture doesn't make sense until someone else helps you draw in the lines.

Squint tugged on my sleeve. "Don't tell anyone, okay?

132

Not even Circe. Jack would . . . well, he'd be awful mad at Sage, and he'd kill the eagle for sure. She's getting better, and maybe when he lets her go, she'll fly away from here."

"I won't tell," I said as I watched her spread her wings toward the sides of the cage. "I promise."

I looked for Circe as we took the path back through the woods but didn't see her.

***

The sun was poking through the scattering clouds by the time we got back to the house. The chickens had come out from their hiding places, scratching around the puddles that were already drying in the yard.

"Where were you?" Colleen asked very slowly, releasing Squint slightly from her hug, then gripping his shoulders as she knelt to look into his eyes. "Are you going to tell us why you made us worry so?"

Circe stood silently against the kitchen doorjamb, winding a towel around her fist.

He didn't answer Colleen, but pulled himself free. She was standing between us. All I could see of his face were his eyes, but they were set on me. I knew he wasn't going to let her know where he'd been. He was waiting for me to answer. He was waiting to see if I'd tell.

Sage came up behind me and placed his hand on the back of my neck. "Yes, Rudy," he said as he moved around in front of me. Up close I could see blood dried in the deep wounds the eagle had made on his arm. "Yes. Tell us where you found the boy."

Jack was in the kitchen by then, and the three adults looked at me, impatient for me to say something.

"He—he was already on his way home when—when I found him. . . ." I stammered. "Circe was there."

133

"I'm sorry," Squint said softly, stepping away from Colleen to stand alone in the middle of the room. "I didn't mean . . . I went . . . I went over the gate." I felt Sage's nervousness run through his hand to my neck. His hold tightened.

"You did what?" Sage's voice boomed across the kitchen.

I could tell Squint wanted to cry, but he let his tears hang on, just barely clinging to the rim of his eyes.

"I went over the gate, . . ." he mumbled, ". . . to the cabin." When he finally cried, it was as if a fissure had opened up inside him, letting the tears spill out. They came with powerful, painful sobs that seemed to take up all the space in the room.

For a moment no one spoke. Colleen started to go to him, but Jack held her back, shaking his head. Then Sage's grip on me began to relax, and he reached for Squint with his free hand. "It's okay, kid. No need to be too hard on yourself. We all make mistakes." He looked down at me then, a hand on each of us, and squeezed gently. "It's only what you do afterwards that you ought to judge yourself by."

Colleen dismissed Squint to go upstairs and take a bath. Then she turned to me. "Rudy, your parents got through again. I think they are starting to believe we don't really have you here at all. I spoke to your dad, and he said he and your mother would be here early tomorrow. Your dad said they'd be in a hurry because he wanted to make a stop on the way home. Something about your grandfather. . . ." Her voice faded as she turned toward the refrigerator to get me something to eat, but the words echoed in my head like stones dropping into a deep well.

Papa D. Tomorrow my parents would make me try to see him again. Suddenly it felt as if we'd just had another earthquake.

Chapter
24

T hat evening after we fed the dogs, I waited by the barn for Circe to lock up. She was more solemn than usual, hardly saying a word except that she'd miss me and Smithers when we were gone. Something was bothering her, but I knew it was more than just TomDog.

As she left the barn, she slid the latch on the gate and turned to look up at the sky. The storm had washed the air so clean I could almost smell new grass poking up through the dampened earth.

Wisps of fog drifted along the ridge above the barn and sank into the treetops. Millions of stars winked on and off behind it. I had forgotten how full of stars the sky could be so far away from the city. Circe set down the bucket and ran her hand backward through her hair.

"I've ruined it." She sighed. "I hurt Squint real bad this afternoon."

Beside me in the dark she seemed suddenly much older than fifteen, and so lonesome it made me ache for her. "I don't think he's mad at you," I said.

"No, he's not mad, but he'll never forgive me for saying I hated the game. Everything's changed. It's over now."

"Come on, Circe. I bet he has already forgotten."

"You just don't understand," she said bitterly, looking away from me toward the woods. She bent over and lifted the empty bucket as if it was made of stone, then headed for the house.

When I caught up to her, I expected her to say something nasty to me, but her eyes were strangely sad. "Some things you just can't do anything about. Uncle Jack was right. When a thing is ruined, it's gone. Like breaking an egg. You can't put the pieces back together."

"Change doesn't always mean ruined," I heard myself say. But she didn't hear me, or didn't listen.

***

The door to the bedroom was partly closed, and the room was in shadows except for the light from the hall window where the moon was shining in. Squint was already asleep, snoring softly. I followed the thin white line of light to my bed across the room.

Maybe she was right, I thought. Maybe you can't put a broken thing back together. But that doesn't mean you have to throw it away, either. You might get something different, but it could be something just as good. The strangest feeling came over me then, as if I'd heard those words inside my head before but never paid attention.

I switched on the light beside the bed and glanced down at the picture of me and Papa D that was still lying where I'd left it. The crease seemed even wider than it had the last time I'd let myself look at it. But in the light of that little lamp, all at once Papa D's expression seemed almost comical. The crease set off his wide white grin and made it broader than it really was. It spread the whole width of his face, and now he just seemed to be laughing at me.

The next day the hounds let us know my parents were coming, long before we could hear the van. They set to howling like the world was about to end, and even Smithers offered his measure of warning.

As Dad pulled up, I tried to see his face to find out if he was angry. But all I could see in the windshield was the reflection of the sky and, as they got closer, the trees and the barn. Finally, the car pulled in front of the house, and when I saw Dad, he was smiling at me like I'd been gone for a hundred years.

Deena and Wade said hello, then hardly gave me a second look before they ran off with Squint to see what the tree had done to the barn.

Fortunately, my dad had the good sense to give me only a pat on the back. But Mom couldn't wait to get her hands on me, and she buried me in a hug that lasted way too long, making me tight inside like I was about to cry.

When she finally set me free, Dad put his hand on my shoulder, and I was sure he was going to lecture me right there in front of everyone. But he said only, "I'm so glad to see you, Son." Then he turned away and gave Smithers a pat on the head.

Dad had not forgotten his camera and didn't waste any time gathering everyone together, lining us all up on the front steps for a picture. I sat beside Squint on the bottom step, with Smithers between us. We both smiled wide grins. Circe was standing behind me so I couldn't see her face, but I hoped she would be smiling too. I didn't want to remember her being sad.

As we got ready to leave, Colleen came from the garden with an armful of roses and handed them to my mother.

"The house looks wonderful," my mom said. "You're working miracles on this old place."

"Yes." Colleen smiled. "I've been plugging away. It's taken a long time, but I think it looks better every day."

I glanced back at the old house with its peeling paint and leaning front porch, and for a moment I could almost see it the way Colleen did—loose boards hammered down, windows reframed, and a fresh coat of yellow paint.

"Say, Jim, how's your father doing?" Jack asked as he and Dad walked toward the car. "Rudy said he suffered a stroke not so long ago."

"Oh, Dad's coming along just fine. His nurse says he's making good progress. Should be in a wheel chair by the end of the week. . . ."

Walking a little behind them, I watched the side of my father's face tighten along his jaw. He was using the same cheerful words he always used when he talked about my grandfather—words that hid the pain and the truth about what was really happening to Papa D.

But they didn't seem to bother me the way they usually did. For the first time I heard the fear behind those words, and I understood he wasn't trying to hide his pain from me. He was hiding it from himself. And I must have been listening to him differently because I wasn't hearing his words as a lie anymore. They began to sound almost like a prayer, as if my father believed that the more often he said them, the closer they'd come to being the truth.

"That's real good news," Jack said, smiling down at my mother. "Is he recognizing anyone yet?"

"No, not yet," said my mom. "I wish there was something we could do to break through. All he needs is to connect somehow. . . ."

"Well, I'm sure he'll be coming around real soon. He's a tough old bird. Missed seeing him this year."